Alex kissed her mouth, taking so much time over it Sarah's heart was pounding when he raised his head. "You know, I'm not so sure about this friend thing after all," he said huskily, his eyes glittering.

She heaved in an unsteady breath, trying to tamp down the heat his expert, hungry mouth had sent surging through her entire body. "You don't want that anymore?"

"Yes, of course I do. But I have a problem."

"What?"

"The way you look tonight, any normal guy would want to be more than just your friend, Sarah. But don't worry," he said softly. "I'll stick to the rules."

"What rules?"

"Yours—friendship with the enemy, but no sleeping with him."

CATHERINE GEORGE was born on the border between Wales and England in a village blessed with both a public and a lending library. Catherine was fervently encouraged to read by a like-minded mother and developed an addiction to reading.

At eighteen Catherine met the husband who eventually took her off to Brazil. He worked as chief engineer of a large gold-mining operation in Minas Gerais, which provided a popular background for several of Catherine's early novels.

After nine happy years the education of their small son took them back to Britain, and soon afterward a daughter was born. But Catherine always found time to read, if only in the bath! When her husband's job took him abroad again she enrolled in a creative-writing course, then read countless novels by Harlequin authors before trying a hand at one herself. Her first effort was not only accepted, but voted best of its genre for that year.

Catherine has written more than sixty novels since and has won another award along the way. But now she has come full circle. After living in Brazil, and in England's the Wirral, Warwick and the Forest of Dean, Catherine now resides in the beautiful Welsh Marches—with access to a county library, several bookshops and a busy market hall with a treasure trove of secondhand paperbacks!

THE MILLIONAIRE'S
REBELLIOUS MISTRESS
CATHERINE GEORGE

~ MISTRESS BRIDES ~

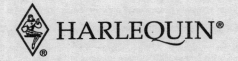

HARLEQUIN®

TORONTO • NEW YORK • LONDON
AMSTERDAM • PARIS • SYDNEY • HAMBURG
STOCKHOLM • ATHENS • TOKYO • MILAN • MADRID
PRAGUE • WARSAW • BUDAPEST • AUCKLAND

Recycling programs
for this product may
not exist in your area.

ISBN-13: 978-0-373-52749-6

THE MILLIONAIRE'S REBELLIOUS MISTRESS

First North American Publication 2010.

Copyright © 2008 by Catherine George.

www.eHarlequin.com

Printed in U.S.A.

THE MILLIONAIRE'S
REBELLIOUS MISTRESS

PROLOGUE

ALEXANDER MERRICK achieved the vice-chairmanship of the Merrick Group before he was thirty, but no one who worked for him was in the slightest doubt that his appointment was due to ability rather than nepotism. They soon found he ran as tight a ship as his father and his grandfather before him, but with a more humanist approach. He had made it clear from day one that the door of his top floor corner office would always be open to any member of staff with a problem, and this particular morning he sat back, ready to listen, when his assistant came in looking gloomy.

'What's up, Greg? Girlfriend stand you up last night?'

'No, Alex.' Not long out of college, Greg Harris still got a buzz from being on first-name terms with his dynamic young boss. 'I just had a phone call. Bad news. Our bid was unsuccessful.'

'*What?*' Alex Merrick shot upright. 'So who the hell got them?'

'I don't know that yet.' Greg cleared his throat. 'I asked my—my friend to let me know the result of the sealed bid right away, as a personal favour, which is why I'm ahead of the game, but no other details yet.'

Alex swore volubly. 'It must be some local builder with friends in high places. He'll probably demolish the Medlar Farm cottages and build God knows what in their place—' He broke off, eyeing his assistant speculatively. 'Is your friend a girl?'

Greg nodded, flushing.

Alex gave him the crooked smile that few people could resist. 'Excellent. Take her out to dinner; charm her into finding out who got the bid. I'll pay.'

CHAPTER ONE

THE VIEW of the sunset over sweeping lawns and tree-fringed lake was so perfect the dining room could have been part of a film set.

Sarah's escort smiled at her in satisfaction. 'You obviously approve of my choice, darling?'

'Of course. Who wouldn't?' But she was surprised by it. Oliver normally wined and dined her in more conservative restaurants, where the *cuisine* was less *haute* than Easthope Court. 'Is this a special occasion?'

His eyes slid away. 'Let's leave explanations until later. Our meal is on its way.'

The waiter set Sarah's entrée in front of her, and with a hint of flourish removed the cover from an offering of such culinary art she looked at the plate in awe, not sure whether she should eat it or frame it. But instead of sharing that with someone who took his food as seriously as Oliver, she asked about his latest triumph in court.

Sarah listened attentively as she ate, made appropriate comments at intervals, but at last laid down her knife and fork, defeated. Artistic creation or not, the meal was so substantial she couldn't finish it.

'You didn't care for the lobster?' asked Oliver anxiously.

'It was lovely, but I ate too much of that gorgeous bread before it arrived.'

He beckoned a waiter over. 'Choose a pudding, then, while I excuse myself for a moment. Cheese as usual for me, Sarah.'

She gave the order and sat back, eyeing her surroundings with interest. The other women present—some young, others not—were dressed with varying success in red-carpet-type couture, but their male escorts were largely on the mature side. Though a younger man at table nearby caught her eye, if only because his head of thick, glossy hair stood out like a bronze helmet among his balding male companions. He raised his glass in smiling toast, and Sarah looked away, flushing, as Oliver rejoined her.

'So what are we celebrating?' she demanded, as he began on a wedge of Stilton.

'Now, you must always remember, Sarah,' he began, 'that I have your best interests at heart.'

Her heart sank. 'Go on.'

Oliver reached out a hand to touch hers. 'Sweetheart, there's a vacancy coming up in my chambers next month. Make me happy; give up this obsession of yours and take the job. With your logical brain I'm sure you'd enjoy legal work.'

Sarah's colour, already high, rose a notch. 'You mean you brought me here just to pitch the same old story? Oliver, I love you very much,' she said with complete truth, 'and I know you care about me, but you really must let me live my life my own way.'

'But I just can't believe it's the right way!' Oliver sat back, defeated. 'I hate to think of you messing about with plaster and paint all day in that slum you bought.'

'Oliver,' she said patiently, 'it's what I do. It's what I know how to do. And I love doing it. I'd be useless—and miserable—as a legal secretary, even in illustrious chambers like yours.'

'But you're obviously not taking care of yourself or eating properly—'

'If you just wanted to feed me before I go back to starving in my garret you needn't have wasted money on a place like this,' she informed him.

'I chose somewhere special because it's my birthday tomorrow,' he said with dignity. 'I hoped you'd enjoy helping me celebrate it.'

'Oh Oliver!' Sarah felt a sharp pang of remorse. 'If you're trying to make me feel guilty you're succeeding. I'm sorry. But I can't take the job. Not even to celebrate your birthday.'

He nodded, resigned. 'Ah, well, it was worth a try. We won't let it spoil our evening. Thank you for the witty birthday card, by the way, but you shouldn't have bought a present.'

'Didn't you like the cravat?'

'Of course I liked it. But it was much too expensive—'

'Nothing too good for my one and only godfather!'

Oliver smiled fondly. 'That's so sweet of you, darling, and of course I'll wear it with pride. But you need to watch your pennies.' He leaned nearer and touched her hand. 'You do know, Sarah, that if you're in need of any kind you only have to ask.'

'Thank you, Oliver, of course I do.' But she'd have to be in dire straits before she would.

As they got up to leave, the man Sarah had noticed earlier hurried to intercept them.

Oliver beamed as he shook the outstretched hand. 'Why, hello there, young man. I didn't know you were here.'

'You were too absorbed in your beautiful companion to notice me, Mr Moore.' He turned to Sarah with a crooked smile. 'Hello. I'm Alex Merrick.'

Quick resentment quenched her unexpected pang of disappointment. And as if his name wasn't enough, something in his smile made it plain he thought Oliver was her elderly—and wealthy—sugar daddy.

'Sarah Carver,' she returned, surprised to see comprehension flare in the piercingly light eyes in an angular face that was striking rather than good-looking.

'Sarah is helping me celebrate my birthday,' Oliver informed him.

'Congratulations! It must be an important one to bring you down from London for the occasion.'

'Not really—unless you count each day as an achievement at my age. I'll be sixty-four come midnight,' said Oliver with a sigh, and made a visible effort to suck in his stomach.

'That's just your prime, sir,' Alex assured him. 'Are you from London, too, Miss Carver?'

'She is originally.' Oliver answered for her. 'But Sarah moved to this part of the world last year. I've been trying to persuade her to return to civilisation, but with no success. She's in property development,' he added proudly.

'Snap. That's partly my bag, too,' Alex told her.

Oliver laughed comfortably. 'Not exactly on the same scale,' he informed Sarah. 'Alex is the third generation of his family to run the Merrick Group.'

'How interesting,' she said coolly, and smiled up at Oliver. 'Darling, it's past my bedtime.'

'Right,' he said promptly, and put his arm round her to lead her away. 'Nice seeing you again, young man. My regards to your father.'

Alex Merrick's eyes travelled from Oliver's arm to Sarah's face with a look that brought her resentment to boiling point. 'I hope we meet again.'

'You weren't very friendly,' commented Oliver in the car park. 'You might do well to cultivate young Alex, darling. The Merrick name carries clout in these parts.'

'Not with me,' Sarah said fiercely.

The journey home was tiring. Oliver returned to his proposition, and argued all the way, but when he paused to draw breath Sarah told him it would turn her life upside down again to move back to London.

'I did all that in reverse not so long ago, Oliver. I don't fancy doing it again for a while, if at all. I like living in the wilds, as you call it—'

'But what do you do with yourself in the evenings, for God's sake?'

Glossing over the weariness which more often than not sent her early to bed with a book, Sarah said something vague about cinema trips and concerts, hoping Oliver wouldn't ask for details.

'A lot different from London,' he commented, as they reached Medlar House.

'Which is entirely the point, Oliver. Would you like some coffee?'

'No, thank you, darling. I'll head straight back to Hereford. I'm meeting with a local solicitor first thing in the morning.'

She leaned across and kissed him. 'Thank you for the wonderful dinner, *and* for the job offer. But do stop worrying about me. I'll be fine.'

'I hope so,' he said with a sigh. 'You know where I am if you need me.'

'I do.' She patted his cheek. 'Happy birthday for tomorrow, Oliver.'

Sarah waved him off, and with a yawn made for her ground-floor retreat in a building which had once housed an elite school for girls. Advertised as a studio flat, when the school had been converted into apartments, she'd agreed to take a look at it without much hope. It had been the last on the list of remotely possible flats shown her by the estate agent, who had rattled through his patter at such speed he'd been unaware that the moment she'd walked through the door Sarah fell in love.

The agent had given her the hard sell, emphasising that it was the last available in her price range in the building, and offered interesting individual touches.

'If you mean a ceiling four metres high and one wall composed entirely of windows,' Sarah remarked. 'Heat loss must be a problem.'

Crestfallen, the young man had informed her that it had

once been a music room, which explained the lofty dimensions, and then he'd pointed out its view of the delightful gardens and repeated his spiel about the building's security. Sarah had heard him out politely, and when he'd eventually run out of steam, he saw her back to her car, promising to ring her in the morning with other possibilities.

She'd forced herself to wait until he rang, praying that no one had beaten her to it overnight with the flat. When his call finally came he'd given her details of a riverside apartment. Way out of her price range, she'd told him, and then as an apparent afterthought mentioned that since there was nothing else suitable on his current list she might as well take another look at the Medlar House bedsit. He'd uttered shocked protests at the term for such a picturesque studio flat, but once they were back in the lofty, sunlit room again Sarah had listed its disadvantages as her opening shot, then begun haggling. At last the agent had taken out his phone to consult a higher authority, and agreement had been reached on a price well below the maximum Sarah had been prepared to pay to live in Medlar House—which, quite apart from its other attractions, was only a short drive from the row of farm cottages she was about to transform into desirable dwellings.

All that seemed a lifetime ago. Feeling restless after her unaccustomed evening out, Sarah loosened her hair, then sat at the narrow trestle table that served as desk, drawing board, and any other function required of it. She booted up her laptop, did a search, and gave a snort of laughter. To say that Sarah Carver and Alexander Merrick were both in property was such a stretch it was ludicrous. These days the Merrick Group also had extensive manufacturing interests, at home and abroad—and the biggest buzzword of all—it was into recycling on a global scale. She closed the laptop in sudden annoyance. It was irrational to feel so hostile still. But the look the man had given her had annoyed her intensely. Oliver was sixty-three—she glanced at her watch—sixty-four now. She was almost forty years his junior. So of course Merrick Mark Three had jumped to the wrong conclusion about Oliver's role in her life. Her eyes kindled. As if she cared.

She went through her night-time routine in her minuscule bathroom, then climbed up to her sleeping balcony and hung up the little black dress she hadn't worn for ages. She got into bed and stretched out to gaze down through the balustrade at the moonlight streaming through the shutters, hoping the lobster wouldn't give her nightmares. She had to be up early next morning, as usual. The first of the cottages was coming along nicely, and once furnished it would function as a show house to tempt buyers for the others in the row. Harry Sollers, the local builder who worked with her, would be there before her, in case, as sometimes happened, he knocked off half an hour early to do a job for a friend.

When the row of cottages had gone up for sale by sealed auction Harry's circle of cronies at his local pub had fully expected some big company to demolish them and pack as many new houses as possible on the site. When the news had broken that a developer from London had snaffled the property there had been much morose shaking of heads in the Green Man—until the landlord had surprised his clients by reporting that the property developer was a young woman, and she was looking for someone local to work on the cottages. At which point Harry Sollers—semi-retired master builder, committed bachelor and misogynist—had amazed everyone in the bar by saying he might be interested.

Sarah never ceased to be grateful that, due to Harry Sollers' strong views on the demolition of perfectly good living accommodation, he'd agreed to abandon semi-retirement to help her turn the one-time farm labourers' cottages into attractive, affordable homes. Gradually Harry had helped her sort out damp courses, retile the roofs, and deal with various basic faults shown up by the building survey. He had been openly sceptical about her own skills until he'd seen proof of them, but openly impressed when he first saw her plastering a wall, and completely won over the day she took a lump hammer to the boards covering up the original fireplaces.

But from the start Harry had drawn very definite lines about his own capabilities, and told Sarah she would need to employ local craftsmen for specialised jobs. He'd enlisted his nephew's experienced help with the cottage roofs, recommended a reliable electrician to do the rewiring, and for the plumbing contacted his friend Fred Carter, who soon proved he was top-of-the-tree at his craft. The houses had begun to look like real homes once the quality fittings were in place, but to his surprise Sarah had informed Fred that she would do the tiling herself, as well as fit the cupboards in both bathrooms and kitchens.

'I'm good at that kind of thing,' she'd assured him, without conceit.

This news had caused a stir in the Green Man.

'You might have to put up with a few sightseers now and again, boss, just to prove Fred wasn't having them on,' Harry had warned her.

He was right. Harry's cronies had come to look. But once they'd seen her at work they'd agreed that the city girl knew what she was doing.

But much as she enjoyed her work there were days when Sarah felt low-key, and the next day was one of them—which was probably due to Oliver and his coaxing about the vacancy in his chambers. It was certainly nothing to do with the lobster, which had not, after all, given her nightmares. Nor, she assured herself irritably, was it anything to do with meeting Alex Merrick. She'd slept well and risen early, as usual. Nevertheless her mood today was dark. She would just have to work through it. Fortunately Harry was never a ray of sunshine first thing in the morning either, and wouldn't notice. But for once she was wrong.

'You're early—and you don't look so clever today,' Harry commented.

'I was out socialising last night,' she informed him, and went on with the cupboard door she was hanging.

His eyebrows shot up. 'Who was the lucky lad, then?'

Sarah sometimes joined Harry for a ploughman's in the Green Man at lunchtime, where the clientele was mainly male. Some of the regulars were retired, and came out for an hour's chat over a pint, but the younger set were mainly tradesmen of varying kinds on their lunch-breaks. Harry had put up with a lot of teasing from the old hands about his pretty young boss, but some of the new ones tried to chat Sarah up. The more enterprising among them had even asked her out, and it had taken all the tact she possessed to refuse in a way that made no dent in local egos, so she could hardly blame Harry for being curious about her night out.

'Much as he'd love to hear himself referred to as a lad,' she said, with her first smile of the day, 'we were celebrating my escort's sixty-fourth birthday. He's in Hereford on business for a couple of days so he drove over to take me to dinner at Easthope Court last night.'

He whistled, impressed. 'I hear it's pretty fancy there since it was done over—pricey too.'

'Astronomically! I could have fed myself for a week on what Oliver paid for my meal last night. He comes down to check up on me now and then, convinced I'm starving myself to death, but usually all he asks of a restaurant is a good steak and a glass of drinkable claret.' Sarah sighed, feeling a sudden need to confide in someone. 'He's a barrister by profession, Harry. He wants me to work in his chambers.'

'Does it need building work, then?'

'No.' Sarah explained about the office job.

'He thought you'd like that?' Harry said, scratching his head. 'Can you do typing and all the computer stuff?'

She nodded. 'After I left college I ran the office at my father's building firm.'

'You did a whole lot more than that, I reckon. Your dad taught you his craft pretty good.'

'Thank you!' Coming from Harry, this was high praise

indeed. 'By the way,' she added casually, 'I met someone called Merrick last night. Do you know him?'

Harry grunted. 'Everybody knows the Merricks. Old Edgar started off in scrap metal. A right old villain he was; so slick at making money you'd think he'd found a way to turn scrap into gold. His son George made an even bigger packet when he took over and started expanding. The family's got a bit gentrified since Edgar's day, with college education and all that. Easthope Court was one of their jobs. Lot of publicity at the time. Was it George you met?'

'No. This one's name was Alex.'

'George's son. Don't know the lad myself, but word has it he's a right ball of fire now he runs the show up here. I hear George is at the London branch these days.' Harry's lined blue eyes gave her a very straight look. 'I hear a lot of things in the pub, boss, but I just listen. Nothing you say to me will go further.'

'No need to tell me that, Harry!'

He nodded, satisfied. 'I'll get on with the window frames in number four, then. You're doing a good job there,' he added gruffly, eyeing the cupboards.

'Thank you!' Sarah smiled at him so radiantly he blinked. 'How about a snack at the Green Man at lunchtime? My treat?'

'You're on! Betty Mason bakes pasties on Wednesdays.'

Sarah felt a lot better as she went on with her cupboard doors. She worked steadily throughout the morning, with only a short break for coffee, and got to her feet at last, back aching. She went to the door, put two fingers in her mouth and gave a piercing whistle.

'Ready, Harry? I'm starving.'

Harry chuckled as she scrambled into his pick-up.

'What's up?' she demanded.

'You don't look much like a city girl these days, boss.'

Sarah grinned as she tucked a stray curl behind her ear. 'The great advantage of the Green Man is not having to prettify myself to eat there. But if you're ashamed to be seen with me in my working clothes, Mr Sollers, I can always eat my pasty in the pick-up.'

He guffawed. 'Get away with you.'

The knot of regulars in the bar greeted Sarah with their usual friendly acceptance, which put paid to the last traces of her blue mood.

'Your boss let you out, then, Harry?' called some comedian.

'Reminded her it was Betty's day for pasties, so I hope you lot left some for us.' Harry hoisted Sarah up on a stool at the bar, and gave their order. Fred came to join them, to ask about their progress, and Sarah willingly obliged as she tucked into flaky pastry wrapped round a savoury mixture of meat and vegetables. When it struck her that she was enjoying it far more than the elegant meal of the night before she sighed in such remorse that Fred peered under the peak of her cap.

'Something wrong with your pasty, my dear?'

'Nothing at all—it's delicious.' She explained about the meal with Oliver.

'The man must have deep pockets if he took you to eat at Easthope Court,' put in another man.

'It was to celebrate his birthday, Mr Baker,' said Sarah, and looked at him speculatively. 'Actually, I'm glad you're here today—'

'He's here every day,' someone shouted.

'But I'm not, so I must grab him while I can,' she called back, grinning. 'I hear you're a very keen gardener, Mr Baker.'

'I do a bit,' he admitted warily.

'When you can spare the time, would you come along to the cottages and give me some advice on planting?'

'Any time you like,' he assured her. 'Let me get you another half.'

'No, thanks—too much to do this afternoon,' she said regretfully.

There was immediate interest in exactly what, and the conversation was general for a moment, until a voice with the accents of expensive education rose above the hubbub to make itself heard to the landlord.

'I'm looking for a Miss Carver, Eddy. Has she been in here today?'

Sarah winced, wishing vainly she could make herself invisible. Resigned, she let Fred help her down from the stool and turned to face Alex Merrick. 'You were asking for me?'

His formal dark suit looked out of place in the homely environs of the Green Man's public bar, but it was his look of blank astonishment that amused Sarah. Last night, because Oliver adored being seen with a 'pretty young thing', as he put it, she'd been tricked out in her best babe outfit, clinging black dress, killer heels, full warpaint and hair swept up in a knot of curls. Today the hair was rammed under a baseball cap, her face was as nature had made it, her overalls and trainers were covered in streaks of paint and glue and without her heels she was four inches shorter. She couldn't blame the man for mistaking her for a boy apprentice, and felt grateful when Harry and Fred ranged themselves alongside her in protective, burly support.

Alex glanced round the watchful faces in the bar, lips twitching. 'Good afternoon, Miss Carver. I didn't recognise you for a moment. My apologies for interrupting your lunch.'

She shrugged. 'Not at all. I was about to get back to work. What can I do for you?'

'I'd like a word—in private. Today, if possible.'

Sarah eyed him speculatively. 'I generally finish about six. I can see you then, if you want.'

'Thank you. Where?'

'At the site. I'm sure you know where it is.'

'I do. Until six, then. Good afternoon, gentlemen.' He gave a comprehensive nod all round and walked out, leaving a brief lull in the conversation behind him before everyone started talking again.

'You want to watch that one,' said Harry.

'Why?' she asked, downing the last of her cider.

'He's a Merrick, for a start.'

No need to remind her of that!

'Besides, you've only got to look at him,' said Fred. 'Fancies his chance with the ladies.'

'Not one dressed like this,' she said, laughing.

'Don't you be too sure of that,' said Fred darkly.

Harry grinned, and drained his glass. 'No need to worry. One swing of her lump hammer and he'll be done for.'

They left the pub to a burst of laughter, but Harry looked thoughtful as he drove back to the site. 'Just the same, boss, I think I'd better stay behind out of sight in one of the cottages tonight. Just in case.'

Sarah stared at him, surprised, 'The man wants to talk to me, that's all.'

'Yes, but what about?' said Harry grimly. 'Word is that the Merricks were none too pleased when you got those cottages.'

'Because they're on land adjoining theirs?'

He nodded. 'So be warned. I reckon young Merrick's going to make you an offer.'

'So he can knock them down?' Sarah's mouth tightened in a way her father would have recognised only too well. 'Not a chance.'

It took work, but she finally persuaded Harry that she would be perfectly all right alone when he left.

'Just the same,' he said, as he got in his pick-up, 'you be careful.'

'I shall keep my trusty hammer close to hand,' she assured him, only half joking.

Once he'd gone, Sarah almost wished she'd asked Harry to stay after all. Which was ridiculous. It was broad daylight on a summer evening. What could happen? She thought about tidying herself up but couldn't be bothered. Mr Alex Merrick would have to take her as she was. She leaned back against her car, arms folded and ankles crossed, blocking out the site's building gear as she studied the cottages objectively. Harry had replaced the gingerbread trim over each front door, and soon he'd begin painting the exterior walls creamy white. The front gardens were just bare patches of earth as yet, but she would plant them up after some advice from Mr Baker. She'd lay some cobbles on the paths, get the waist-high dividing walls repointed, and once the lawns had been sown with seed...

She turned her head as a Cherokee Jeep cruised down the lane.

Alex Merrick sprang down from it, but instead of jumping to attention Sarah stayed leaning against her car.

'Hello,' he said, smiling. 'I'm a few minutes late. Thank you for waiting. I got held up.'

'I didn't notice the time,' Sarah said with complete truth.

'Because you were lost in rapt contemplation of your work. Understandable,' he said, looking along the row. 'The houses look good.'

'Thank you. So why do you need to speak to me, Mr Merrick?' she asked, cutting straight to the chase.

The smile vanished. 'I could have done this officially, requested a meeting at my office, but it's probably better to talk here on site. What are your plans when the houses are finished?'

'Why do you ask?'

'Professional interest,' he said briefly.

She eyed him warily. 'I shall put them up for sale to first-time buyers, or city dwellers with a fancy for a bolthole in the country.'

'I can save you the trouble.' He took in the cottages with a sweep of his hand. 'On behalf of the Merrick Group I'll buy all six from you—if the price is right.'

She stood erect at last, eyeing him with suspicion. 'What for, exactly?'

Alex Merrick frowned, as though he couldn't believe she wasn't overwhelmed with delight. 'The usual reasons, Miss Carver.'

'I'd like to know exactly what they are, just the same. Because the land they stand on borders yours you might have demolition in mind—in which case nothing doing.'

His eyebrows snapped together. 'I assure you that provided they meet with Merrick standards I want them as they are. May I take a look?'

'Of course. Follow me.'

Sarah felt rather like a new mother showing off her baby as Alex followed her inside the first house. She'd done nothing about her own appearance, but she'd gone on a whirlwind tour of all the houses with broom and cleaning rags, determined to present them at their best in the evening sunlight pouring through the windows.

She found she was holding her breath as Alex inspected the kitchen in the first cottage, but in the sitting room she relaxed a little as he nodded in approval at the horseshoe fire-grate gleaming like ebony under its creamy marble mantle. 'Original feature, Miss Carver?'

'Yes, but not the genuine Victorian article, of course. It's a copy, dating from the twenties, like the houses. The fireplaces were boarded up before I rescued them,' Sarah told him. 'The sitting rooms were a bit dark, so we replaced the original windows with French doors to give access to the back courtyards. Some of the flagstones out there were already *in situ,* and I found more in a reclamation yard. After a check with building regulations I removed the dividing walls between the kitchens and dining rooms. Fortunately they were neither party walls nor load bearing, so I achieved more space and light, and at the same time catered to the current preference for combined cooking/eating areas.'

'Good move.' He followed her upstairs to inspect the small bathroom Sarah had created by stealing a sliver of space from the main bedroom.

'There were no bathrooms in the houses originally, of course, just the downstairs lavatory I replaced with a small cloakroom,' she told him, finding his silence oppressive.

'You've utilised all the space very cleverly,' he said at last, 'and installed high-end fittings. Very wise. Which firm did your plumbing?'

'When I embarked on the project I made a conscious

decision to use local craftsmen, and I had the most enormous stroke of luck when master builder Harry Sollers agreed to work with me. He knows all the local tradesmen. He recommended an electrician for the wiring, and introduced me to his friend, Fred Carter, a semi-retired plumber who installed the fittings. But I did all the tiling, and I installed the cupboards in the kitchens and bathrooms myself.'

He shot her a startled look as they returned to the kitchen. 'This is your work throughout?'

She nodded. 'I stripped and sealed the wood floors, and plastered all the inside walls, too, but I asked Harry to paint them because his finish is so superb.'

'But you did the plastering?' he repeated blankly.

'Yes. Next I'm going to tackle the gardens.'

'You found someone local to help you with those, too?'

Sarah nodded. 'But only to do the digging once all the building site gear is cleared away. I need advice on what to plant and where, but I'll do the rest myself.'

When they were outside in the lane Sarah could tell that Alex Merrick looked back at the row of cottages with new eyes.

'So what do you think?' she couldn't help asking.

'I'm impressed. Congratulations on your achievement.' His manner suddenly changed. 'So, Miss Carver, I repeat my offer. If your terms are realistic I'll buy the lot, but I want the houses ready to inhabit on the day of completion, also cleared parking space at either end of the row. So name your figure.'

Sarah shook her head. 'Impossible right away. I can't say to the day when the cottages will be completely ready, and costs may increase before I can get them valued.' And, much more important than that, no way would she sell to a Merrick.

'If you hang about too long, Miss Carver, the offer may no longer be on the table.' His eyes, which had opalescent grey irises with dark rims, which gave them an unsettling intensity, held hers. 'Have a chat about it with Oliver Moore. I assume he's your financial backer?'

Her jaw clenched. 'No, he's not, Mr Merrick. His sole involvement in my project is on legal matters.'

He raised an eyebrow. 'A bit minor league for a Queen's Counsel!'

'But not for the local solicitor Oliver found for me.' She turned away. 'Now, I'd like to get home, Mr Merrick. I'm tired and dirty—'

'And hungry? In that case let's discuss the deal in more detail later over dinner,' he said promptly.

'No, thank you.'

'Another time, maybe? Contact me when the houses are finished.' He reached for his wallet and took out a card. 'Here's my office address and my various phone numbers.'

Sarah tucked it into a pocket without looking at it. 'I'm surprised you came yourself, Mr Merrick. Surely you pay people to do this kind of thing for you?'

'True. But after meeting you last night it seemed best to sort it myself.' He smiled crookedly. 'Though I confess I didn't recognise you in the pub today.'

'I could tell.' She walked round the car and got in.

His eyebrows rose as he glanced down at the passenger seat. 'Do you always carry a lump hammer round with you?'

'Only when I'm meeting strange men.'

'Nothing strange about me,' he assured her. 'Where do you live?'

'Medlar House,' she said, and started the car. 'Goodbye.'

Sarah drove up the lane and out on to the main road, grinding her teeth in frustration when a look in the mirror confirmed that Alex Merrick was following her home. When he'd parked the Cherokee on the forecourt beside her car he jumped out, holding up his hands in mock surrender.

'I come in peace! But seriously, Miss Carver,' he added, 'forget the deal for a minute. I would very much like to take you out to dinner. Unless Oliver Moore would object?' he added, then cursed his mistake as her eyes flashed under the peak of her cap.

'Nothing doing,' Sarah said flatly.

He frowned. 'Why not?'

'Last night, Mr Merrick, your thought processes were insultingly obvious, just because I was dining in an expensive restaurant with a man old enough to be my father.' Her chin lifted. 'But in the unlikely event that I did socialise with you Oliver would actually approve, because he knows you—or knows your family. I'm not Oliver Moore's bit of fluff, Mr Merrick. He's my godfather.'

CHAPTER TWO

ALEX cursed under his breath as he watched the small figure march into the building. He'd noticed her the moment she entered the restaurant last night. Big dark eyes, and a full-lipped mouth just a shade too wide for her face had attracted his attention early on. And not only because her companion was a barrister his father knew. The age gap between the pair had convinced the cynic in Alex that she was Oliver Moore's trophy girlfriend, whereas in actual fact Sarah Carver was something of a surprise package. How she'd managed to pull a fast one with the sealed bid was still a mystery.

Greg Harris's useful girlfriend had soon learned who'd acquired the Medlar Cottages site, and passed on the information that the unknown Miss Carver intended renovating and restoring the cottages instead of demolishing them to build on the land. At which point Alex had instructed a manager in one of the group's subsidiary firms to make an offer for the site and cottages as they were. When it was turned down flat Alex had decided to sit back and let Miss Carver do exactly what he'd intended for the houses in the first place. Regular checks would be made on their progress, and then, when they were nearing completion, he would simply step in and make his bid for the lot. Decision made, the small, relatively unimportant venture had been relegated to a back burner—until he'd run into Sarah with Oliver Moore at last night. At which point it had shot straight to the top of his priority list.

At Easthope Court Sarah Carver had appealed to him strongly in that sexy black dress, yet today, minus make-up and plus a layer of dust, she'd somehow managed to look equally appealing in her working clothes. She'd made no attempt to tidy up to meet him tonight, not even to wash her dirty face. His mouth tightened. He was accustomed to women who polished themselves to a high gloss for him, while Sarah Carver obviously didn't care a damn what he thought of her. Suddenly he felt an urge to strip those grubby overalls from her curvy little body and— His mind stopped dead as his hormones prodded him. Watch it, Merrick. Stick to the rules. Never mix business with pleasure.

Alex strolled over to the imposing front door of the school he'd known quite well when he was a teenager. He'd come here for dances in the old days, and had fond memories of some hot and heavy necking in concealed corners when the chaperones weren't looking. And, because the Merrick Group had converted the building into pricey flats, he was in a position to know that Miss Sarah Carver could hardly be penniless if she owned one of them. Unless Oliver Moore had bought it for her. Alex found her name on the row of doorbells, considered pushing it, then shrugged and went back to the Cherokee. To hell with it. He'd ring Sarah's bell some other night. One way or another.

Sarah cursed herself and Alex Merrick in the same breath once she was safe in her flat. In her rush to escape him she'd forgotten to shop on the way home. Even more annoying, she'd half expected him to ring the bell the moment she was inside, and felt an irritating sense of anti-climax when it didn't happen. She shrugged angrily. Forget him and think supper. It was a long time since her pasty with Harry. But first on the agenda, as always, she needed a shower.

After that she rang Oliver to wish him happy birthday, thanked him again for the meal at Easthope Court, and finally made for her narrow, high-ceilinged kitchen. She concocted a rarebit from an elderly piece of cheese and the last of her bread, and carried the tray over to the window seat she'd built with her own hands to curve round the bay which formed half the windows. The materials had come from the building supply merchant who'd put her in touch with Harry Sollers; a stroke of luck she gave thanks for daily.

Sarah looked out on the gardens as she ate—something she did every evening when the sun shone, and most times when it didn't. A double row of white-painted shutters controlled the flood of natural light, and even just watching the rain pour down on lawns and trees was relaxing. Her mother had done the gardening in their North London house, but after Louise Carver died her grieving husband had been too involved in comforting his inconsolable daughter while trying to keep his failing business afloat to maintain the garden to his wife's standard. Sam Carver had been adamant about fulfilling his wife's wish to send their daughter to college, even when Sarah had fought tooth and nail against the idea and pleaded to work for her father straight from school. In the end she'd given in, but had taken a Business Studies course instead of her original intention to study art and design. And after classes and at weekends she'd worked with the construction crew and pulled her weight.

To please her father she'd socialised with girls from college occasionally, but had felt happier in the company of the bricklayers and carpenters, electricians and plumbers she'd known all her life. The old hands had treated her like one of the boys, but when nature had finally added curves to her shape, some of the newer, younger ones had begun treating her very much as a girl. It was a new phase which had added considerably to her father's worries, as Sarah had gone out several nights a week with one young man or another.

'It's all right, Dad, safety in numbers,' she'd assured him when he had commented on it. 'I'm having fun, nothing heavy. They're just friends.'

'They're also men,' he'd warned her. 'So watch your step.'

But once she'd left college to manage the firm's offices, it had been Sarah's turn to worry when Sam Carver had grown older and greyer before her eyes, losing contracts to bigger outfits. She had put her social life on hold to stay home to cook proper meals every evening, and to share them with her father to make sure he ate them. Eventually, it had been during one of those meals that Sam had faced Sarah across the table and told her he'd had an offer from Barclay Homes for the firm.

'*No!* You're selling it?' she said, appalled.

'Yes, I am, Sarah,' he said heavily. 'At least this way we'll salvage something out of it.'

Horrified, Sarah argued that they should carry on, *must* carry on, but Sam was unshakeable.

'I've made up my mind, pet. I had a chat with the Barclay Homes manager, and there's a job for you in their local branch if you want it. Though if you don't you should find a job anywhere now, with your experience in the building trade. But I'm jacking it in.'

She swallowed her tears and clutched him tightly. 'But, Dad, what will you do?'

'Retire,' he said, patting her. 'I've been running on empty for a while now, my darling, I need a rest.'

'But I don't want to work for someone else,' she cried, then, shamed by her whining, managed a smile. 'But of course I will. And a job with Barclay Homes means I can live at home with my dad.' And look after him.

Within days the contract was signed and Sarah was given an interview with the manager of Barclay Homes. The night before her start in the new job she made a special dinner to share with her father, and tried not to worry when he ate so little. Afterwards she drank coffee with him in the garden in the warm twilight, relieved to see him looking relaxed for the first time in months as he stretched out in a deckchair.

'I'll be able to get your mother's garden in proper shape

now,' he said later, yawning. 'You should have an early night, pet, to make sure you're on top form in the morning. I think I'll stay out here in the cool for a while.'

Knowing it was where he felt closest to her mother, Sarah bent and kissed him, told him not to be too late, then went up to bed. When she woke in the night and found his bed hadn't been slept in Sarah ran downstairs, panicking, and raced barefoot into the garden to find Sam Carver still in his deck-chair, fast asleep. Scolding, she hurried to shake him awake, then let out a cry of raw anguish when she realised he would never wake again.

The following period remained a blur in Sarah's mind. The only thing constant had been the solid presence of her mother's cousin, Oliver Moore. Like a rock in her sea of grief, he had seen to all the arrangements, and supported her through the well-attended funeral. Sam Carver had been a popular employer, and it had seemed to Sarah that anyone who had ever worked for her father had turned up to pay their respects. Financially Sarah was well provided for. Her mother had left a sum of money in trust for her, and this security, together with the proceeds from the sale of the business and the sum expected for the large, well-maintained house in a sought-after North London location, had given Sarah breathing space to consider her future.

But constantly keeping the house up to inspection stan-dards had been tiring on top of a day's work, and living alone in it had been hard. Keeping strictly to office work in her new job had been even harder. She'd missed the camaraderie of the building site. The final blow had come when the family home had finally been sold and she'd had to find somewhere else to live. When two office colleagues had offered her a room in their flat she'd jumped at the chance, glad of their friendly company, but her Sundays had usually been spent with Oliver. He liked to drive her into the country and feed her substantial meals at some inn he'd seen reviewed in the

Sunday papers, and during one of their trips they'd come across the Medlar Farm cottages. At first glance she'd thought they were part of a Merrick Group hotel site, but when she'd found they were up for sale by auction Sarah had known at once how she wanted to spend her inheritance. Oliver had objected strongly at first, but eventually bowed to the inevitable by paying a building surveyor to value the houses and confirm that they were worth buying. When Oliver had been informed that the cottages were sound and the auction was to be sealed bid, he'd advised Sarah that if she were really determined she should bid slightly more than the properties were considered worth.

Sarah had taken his advice, confident that her father would have approved. Her euphoria when her bid was successful had gone a long way to reassuring Oliver, but he'd had serious qualms when she'd immediately resigned from her job. His reaction to the one-room 'studio' flat had been equally gloomy, but Sarah had been adamant that it was a good investment. The former school building had charm, and she'd assured him that she was more than capable of making the flat so inviting she would make a tidy profit on it when she came to sell.

But now she'd knocked it into shape she didn't want to sell it. Sarah frowned as she looked round her lofty, uncluttered space. After working on the flat practically every evening since she'd moved in, she was at a loose end now it was finished. But the cure for that was easy enough. She'd spend the long, light evenings working in the cottage gardens instead, and at night pore over gardening magazines instead of the building manuals and style publications she'd studied while doing up the cottages. And maybe, just maybe, she'd say yes some time if one of the likely lads at the Green Man asked her out.

Having fully expected Alex Merrick to hound her over the purchase of Medlar Cottages, Sarah was surprised—and rather nettled—to be proved wrong. She heard nothing more from him, and assumed that the offer from the Merrick Group, just as he'd warned, was no longer on the table. Not that it mattered.

'That's a ferocious frown, lass,' said Harry, as he climbed down a ladder. 'Something wrong?'

'I haven't put the cottages up for sale yet, but I can't help wondering how well—and how soon—they'll sell when I do.'

'Don't you worry. You'll have no trouble selling this lot,' he said with certainty. 'They're attracting a lot of attention locally. Mind, it doesn't hurt that the developer's a pretty young female—'

'Harry, are you by any chance being sexist?' she accused.

'If I was you'd sack me,' he said, chuckling, then shook his head as a van came cruising up the lane. 'More visitors,' he grumbled. 'I reckon we should start selling tickets.'

Sarah's eyes lit up. 'It's Mr Baker.'

Charlie Baker heaved himself out of the van and came to look at the houses in approval. 'Morning, Miss Carver, Harry. I've brought the plants you wanted, my dear, and a few bags of compost to get you started.'

Sarah rushed to inspect the plants, and helped the men carry everything to the parking space cleared at the end of the row. 'Lavender for fragrance and buddleia for butterflies,' she said, delighted. 'My mother's favourites.'

'I brought you some viburnums and a couple of hollies, too,' he told her. 'No point in putting in bedding plants, otherwise you'd be down here every night watering.'

'I'm not really clued up about gardening. I wish now I'd helped my mother more in our garden at home,' said Sarah with regret. 'I was always making a nuisance of myself on one of Dad's building sites instead.'

'It paid off,' Harry reminded her. 'Now, we'd better get back to the real work. I want to finish painting number six today.'

'Thank you so much, Mr Baker,' said Sarah as she paid him.

He handed her a receipted bill in exchange. 'Come down the pub some time and I'll buy you that drink.'

'Done,' she said, as they walked back to his van, 'By the way, I was wondering about some trees.'

Harry grinned as he waved at the tree-lined lane. 'Plenty of those here already, boss.'

She made a face at him. 'I meant a smallish flowering tree in the courtyard, and maybe another in the front. What do you think, Mr Baker?'

'I'll bring some catalogues to the pub and you can have a look,' he promised.

Later, when Harry had finished for the day, Sarah waited until his pick-up was out of sight, then, feeling ridiculously furtive, took her mother's garden tools from the boot of her car. It wouldn't take long to plant some of the shrubs in front of what would be the show house. Now that the machinery and skips of rubbish had been hauled away and the parking spaces at either end of the row were clear, the site was beginning to shape up as a very attractive proposition. It was also a mere half a mile to the bus stop on the main road, and only another five to Hereford; a selling point Sarah intended to stress when the houses were advertised.

When her doorbell rang later that evening Sarah's eyes widened as she heard Alex Merrick's voice on the intercom.

'It's very late, Mr Merrick,' she said coldly.

'I wouldn't disturb you if it wasn't important,' he assured her. 'I need a word.'

Thankful she'd bothered to get dressed after her shower for once, Sarah pressed the release button for the main door, then opened her own as he strode across the hall, hand outstretched.

'Thank you for seeing me.'

Sarah touched the hand briefly, but, startled by the contact, dropped it like a hot coal. 'You'd better come inside,' she said—with reluctance, he acknowledged with a twitch of his lips.

Looking disturbingly tougher and more formidable in jeans, and a sweatshirt which showed off impressive shoulders, Alex walked into the room and stood stock still, his eyes wide instead of showing their usual narrow gleam. 'I don't remember anything like this!'

'You mean when your company did the makeover?'

He gave her the crooked smile Sarah felt sure he practised in the mirror.

'I was thinking more of the old days, Miss Carver. My school socialised with the Medlar House girls. I used to come here to dances.'

Of course he had. 'I believe this was a music room.'

'Is that why you have a balcony?'

'No. It's a sleeping platform I built myself. The flight of steps as well. Once I'd sanded and sealed the floor I built the windowseat, too, and installed the shutters,' Sarah couldn't help adding. 'The room was originally just an empty shell with huge windows—plus a tiny kitchen and bathroom, of course, or I wouldn't have bought it.'

Alex looked round slowly, taking in the art nouveau chandelier, the trio of antique mirrors on the wall and the framed family photographs hung between them. 'It's a uniquely attractive room,' he said, with gratifying respect. 'I congratulate you.'

'Thank you. Perhaps you'd like to sit down and tell me why you want to see me?' She returned to her perch on the windowseat.

Alex sat on the edge of the small sofa, his expression grave enough to worry her. 'I took a detour past the cottages tonight on my way home.'

Sarah stared at him in surprise. 'Do you often do that?'

'I do sometimes, to get away from traffic. But tonight I had a different reason. As you know, we're building a spa-type hotel on the site of the old Medlar Farm, a couple of miles from your project. Don't worry,' he added, 'it's not high-rise. It's designed to look organic, blend into the environment. It won't affect your property—particularly if you agree to sell me your cottages.'

'I see. So is there a problem?'

He nodded. 'Security. Late this evening someone got into

our night watchman's cabin at the hotel site while he was on his rounds. He heard a car drive off, and got back to find the Portakabin vandalised.'

'Did they get away with anything?'

'One small television—the solitary thing worth taking. The place was probably trashed in frustration, or just for the sake of it.' Alex looked grim. 'From now on two men with dogs will be on permanent night duty at the site. I drove back via Medlar Cottages, to see if you'd arranged any security there.'

'No,' she said unhappily, 'I haven't.' She brightened. 'But the problem's easy enough to solve. The first house is ready to live in, so I'll move in there until the others are finished.'

Alex gave her a patronising look. 'And what if someone decided to break in one fine night?'

'I'll spread the word in the pub that it's inhabited,' she said promptly. 'Then with the security lights and burglar alarms functioning I'll be fine.'

He shook his head. 'Your decision. But I don't like it.'

'You don't have to like it,' she pointed out.

'I know,' he said morosely, and stood up. 'Give me your mobile phone.'

'Why?'

He held out an imperative hand.

Sarah took the phone from her holdall and handed it to him. 'It's charged and working,' she assured him.

He keyed in some numbers. 'Ring me anytime if you need me, or just feel worried,' he ordered, handing it back. 'Make sure you lock up behind me. Goodnight.'

Sarah glared, incensed, at the door he closed behind him. What earthly right did the man have to come ordering her about? Being fast-tracked to group vice-chairman so young had obviously gone to his head. Damn him for disrupting her life. The last thing she wanted was to move into one of the cottages. Until Alex Merrick had shown up tonight she'd been quite pleased with herself. The cottages were well on schedule, and she was likely to make a sizeable profit on the sale. But now she would have trouble sleeping tonight.

Next morning Sarah was waiting in the lane when Harry arrived. 'Good morning. Could you do me a big favour?'

'Depends, boss,' he said, with a smile which would have surprised his cronies at the pub. 'What do you want?'

She told him about Alex's visit, and the reason for it. 'I haven't given much thought to security,' she said, depressed. 'So I'll just have to move into number one for the time being. Will you cart my sofabed down here in the pick-up, please?'

'No,' said Harry, so flatly Sarah eyed him in dismay.

'But, Harry, I'll never sleep at the flat for thinking someone might be breaking in down here and wrecking the place.'

'And you'll sleep better here on your own? What good would a little thing like you do if someone did break in?' he growled.

Sarah pushed her cap back on her head. 'I'll be straight with you, Harry, I can't afford a security firm.'

He gave it some thought. 'I'd offer to move in myself,' he said at last, 'but better I get Ian to sleep here, bring his dog.'

Her eyes lit up at the thought of the young giant who'd helped with the roofing. 'Would Ian do it?'

'Slip him a few quid and he'll jump at it. He shares a bedroom with his kid brother at home, so he'll be glad of some space for a bit. And he's nearer to his current job here. You've got a kettle, and the fridge is working, so with his portable telly and Nero for company he'll be in clover.'

'We need to fetch my sofabed just the same, then.'

Harry laughed. 'Ian's six foot five in his socks, boss. He'd have your sofa in bits. He can bring his camping gear.' He looked at his watch. 'I'll give him a ring when he's on his break.'

'And while you're at it could you ask Peter Cox to spare us a minute some time today, to make sure the security lights and alarms are all working?' said Sarah.

'Stop worrying, boss. I'll see to it all.'

Ian Sollers was only too happy to do a bit of easy moonlighting, as long as Miss Carver didn't mind Josie coming round of an evening to watch telly with him.

'The girlfriend,' said Harry, reporting. 'Nice kid, Josie.' His lips twitched. 'And if the youngsters get a bit wrapped up in themselves there's always Nero to keep watch for intruders. He's a German Shepherd, and a big lad—like his master.'

Once the security lights and alarms had been checked and confirmed in perfect working order Sarah finally relaxed enough to laugh when Harry teased her about her clandestine gardening.

'You must have started before I was down the lane.'

'I was dying to see how the plants would look.'

'They look good.' He shook his head. 'But it doesn't seem right, a lass like you with nothing better to do with her evenings than grub about in the garden.'

'It makes a change from the carpentry and painting I did every evening until I got my flat sorted—' She broke off as her phone rang.

'I'll make some tea while you answer that,' said Harry, getting up.

'Miss Carver?'

'Yes.'

'Greg Harris here, personal assistant to Alex Merrick. He asked me to let you know that one of our security men will take a drive out to the Medlar Farm Cottages at regular intervals tonight, so there's no need for you to sleep there.'

Sarah rolled her eyes. No use losing her cool with the monkey, she'd wait until she met the organ-grinder again. 'Thank Mr Merrick for me, but I've made my own arrangements. Please pass the message on to his security people.'

'Are you sure about this, Miss Carver?'

'I beg your pardon?' she said icily.

'I mean, after what happened last night I hope you're not going to sleep there yourself after all—'

'I repeat, Mr Harris,' she snapped, 'I've made my own arrangements. Goodbye.'

Mindful of Harry's words about young people getting wrapped up in themselves, Sarah took time to hang curtains at the windows of the show house to give them some privacy. Her plan for decorating a cottage of this era was to keep it simple, with quality curtain material and a rug in muted colours on the gleaming wood floor in the sitting room. When the house was ready for the public she would transfer some of the furniture she'd put in storage, hang a picture or two, and the cottage would look so good she would hate to part with it.

Sarah stood in the doorway of the sitting room, which looked different already with just the addition of curtains and a few things she'd brought from the flat. Much as she resented his high-handedness, Alex Merrick's warnings had given her a wake-up call. It was only common sense from a security point of view to make the house at least appear inhabited.

She heard Harry coming down a ladder and went out to beckon him inside.

'What do you think?'

He whistled. 'Very cosy!'

'Will it con a would-be intruder?'

'No matter. Nero will start barking long before anyone gets near enough to take a closer look.'

Sarah drove back to the flat that evening in high spirits. Ian had turned up in his van with his handsome dog before she left. After a few rapturous minutes spent in making Nero's acquaintance, Sarah had talked money with Ian, and assured the young giant that his Josie was welcome to join him any time.

'Thanks, I appreciate that Miss Carver. But she's at her kickboxing class tonight so I just brought my telly for company.' Ian had looked round with deep approval. 'Josie will love it here. I wish we could afford one of these.'

When Sarah's doorbell rang very late she pulled on her dressing gown and climbed down from her platform, stiffening when she heard the angry, clipped tones of Alex Merrick over the intercom. She buzzed him in, and smothered a snort of laughter as he came storming across the hall in his shirt-sleeves, hair on end, and a great tear flapping in one expensive trouser leg.

'I'm glad you think this is funny! Why the hell didn't you tell me?' he demanded, advancing on her with such menace Sarah had to force herself to stand her ground.

'Good evening, Mr Merrick. Come inside before you wake my neighbours. What should I have told you?'

'That you'd sold one of the cottages,' he snapped.

'I haven't. Harry Sollers' nephew Ian is doing me a favour by sleeping there, that's all. I made it perfectly clear to your Mr Harris that I had my security arrangements in hand,' she added frostily.

Alex controlled himself with obvious difficulty. 'He relayed the message, but it obviously lost something in translation. I took it for granted you were sticking to your plan of sleeping there yourself. I was at a charity dinner earlier, and went home by way of Medlar Cottages to check on you. I got savaged by a bloody great monster of a dog for my pains.'

'That was just Nero, doing his job. Did he bite you?' she asked solicitously.

'No. I fought him off.' Alex glared at the ragged tear. 'I was fond of this suit.'

'If you'll tell me how much it cost I'll reimburse you,' she said promptly, and won a look of such blazing antagonism she backed away a little.

'I didn't come here for money,' he snapped.

'What, then?'

The angular, good-looking face hardened. 'I should think that's obvious,' he snapped, and started towards her.

CHAPTER THREE

SARAH BACKED away in such knee-jerk rejection Alex glared at her, incensed.

'For God's sake, I'm not in the habit of hitting women!' He controlled himself with obvious effort. 'My sole aim was to make sure you came to no harm, alone in one of those cottages. If you'd had the courtesy to let me know what you'd arranged all this nonsense could have been avoided.'

She took in a deep breath. 'I suppose you feel I made a fool of you?'

'Not at all. I made a fool of myself,' he said bitterly, and turned to go.

'Have some coffee first,' she offered, surprising herself as much as Alex. 'You look a bit shaken.'

'Is it any wonder?' he demanded morosely. 'I've never thought of myself as a coward—dammit, I love dogs. But that one scared the hell out of me.'

She felt an unexpected pang of remorse. 'Please have some coffee. Sit there for a minute and relax while I make it.'

When she got back with a couple of mugs Alex was looking round the room, frowning.

'It seems emptier in here tonight.'

'I took a few things down to the cottage for Ian. He provided his own bedroll, plus a couple of garden chairs and a television.' She smiled demurely as she sat on the windowseat with her mug. 'On future evenings his girlfriend Josie will be keeping him company, but tonight she was at her kickboxing class.'

'Kickboxing?' Alex stared at her in horror. 'Then thank God I missed *her*, if she's as big as the boyfriend.'

'I don't know. I hope not.'

'Frightening thought,' he agreed, and drank deeply. 'This is wonderful coffee. Thank you.'

'The least I could do. Though a shot of caffeine is probably the last thing you need right now.'

'It hits the spot just the same.' He yawned suddenly. 'Sorry. I don't suppose I could have a refill?'

Sarah eyed him doubtfully. 'Is that wise?'

'Probably not.' He heaved himself up, but she waved him back and took his mug.

When she returned with the coffee Alex gave her a speculative look. 'This is a very attractive flat, but it's obviously the home of a single woman.' His eyes followed her as she crossed to her windowseat. 'That must surely be from choice?'

Her chin lifted. 'It is.'

'And you obviously think it's none of my business! Though I already know you don't lack for male admirers, Miss Carver,' he added wryly. 'The day I came looking for you it was like trying to detach Snow White from the Seven Dwarfs—only you're the small one. Those pals of yours may be getting on a bit, but they're a hefty bunch.'

Sarah unbent a little. 'I'm a constant source of entertainment to them. In the beginning they were thunderstruck, because I was doing some of the work myself. They kept popping round to check up on the city girl.'

Alex laughed, his eyes dancing in a way which put her on her guard. This man was dangerous.

'I suppose they think it's an unsuitable job for a woman?' Alex commented. 'How did you get into it?'

'My father was a building contractor. I was brought up on

building sites, so I'm doing what I like best and hopefully making a living out of it.'

'With no distractions allowed.' He smiled wryly. 'Once you put me right about your relationship with Oliver Moore, I wondered if you'd shut yourself away in your ivory tower here to mend a broken heart.'

Sarah gave him a scornful look. 'Even if I had it would be none of your business, Mr Merrick.'

But damned interesting, thought Alex, wondering just what there was about this girl that got under his skin. Right now her narrow face was scrubbed and shiny, her hair—the colour of bitter chocolate instead of the blonde he normally preferred— was a tangle of unruly curls. And her pink dressing gown was elderly and faded, and a shade too small, even for someone of her size, which probably meant she'd had it for years but couldn't bear to part with it.

Sarah decided to give him a hint by relieving him of his coffee cup, and he promptly stood up.

'Time I was leaving.'

'I'm sorry about your near-death experience with Nero,' said Sarah, on her way to the door. Though she wasn't in the slightest.

He paused, giving her the crooked smile she was surprised to find she was beginning to find attractive, whether he practised it or not. 'You may laugh, but it wasn't at all funny at the time.'

'No, indeed. And you ruined your suit—or Nero did.'

'No point in sending him a bill, either. Nor,' he added quickly, 'will I send one to you, Miss Carver. I shall write tonight off to experience. Thanks for the coffee.'

'The least I could do after you'd risked life and limb to make sure I was safe,' she assured him, and eyed him curiously. 'But why did you feel you had to?'

'Because I want the cottages. I had to make sure they wouldn't be vandalised,' he lied.

'I see. By the way, did Nero actually hurt you?'

Alex shook his head and raised a muscular leg to show her

an unmarked shin through the rip. 'I had a fight to detach him from my bespoke suiting, but he stopped short of actually savaging me.'

'So no worry about rabies, then?'

He blenched. 'Good God! I hadn't thought of that.'

She eyed him with derision. 'You're in no danger from an aristocrat like Nero.'

'Just the same,' he said with feeling, ' I'll give your property a wide berth from now on—at night, at least.'

'Very wise.' She opened the door, but Alex seemed in no hurry to leave.

'How about changing your mind?' he asked casually.

'About what, exactly?'

'Having dinner with me one evening. We could just talk business, if that would make the idea more attractive.' He listened to himself in disbelief. This kind of persuasion wasn't his style. Probably because he'd never had to use any.

'No—thank you,' she said distantly.

His jaw clenched. 'Why not? Do you find me repulsive?'

'No.'

'Then have you sworn off men as some kind of vow?'

Instead of saying *Just you, Alex Merrick,* as she yearned to, Sarah shook her head. 'I'm just not socialising with anyone right now.'

'Except Oliver Moore,' he reminded her.

'That's right.' She smiled sweetly. 'After all, he is my godfather.'

'So you said.' Alex moved closer, struck by sudden compassion. 'Are you still in mourning for your father? Surely he would want you to get on with your life?'

Sarah's smile vanished. 'As I keep pointing out, my life is my concern, and no one else's, Mr Merrick.'

'Message received,' he said stiffly. 'Goodnight, Miss Carver.'

Sarah felt very thoughtful as she climbed back up to bed later. If she were honest, and she tried hard to be most of the time, she knew she should have told Greg Harris that she'd arranged a night watchman for the cottages. But Alex's high-handed message had really ticked her off. Though he'd certainly paid for it. Sarah grinned at the thought of the vice-chairman of the Merrick Group fighting off a large German Shepherd.

But what had actually sent Alex storming round here afterwards? He'd been so blazingly angry when she'd opened the door to him Sarah had felt a thrill of apprehension, afraid for a split second that he'd throw her on the floor and take his revenge in the time-honoured way. He'd certainly been hot to vent his rage in some way on the person responsible for his clash with Nero. But she hadn't known he'd check up on her himself—had she? Sarah thought about it, and reluctantly admitted that she'd been aware of the possibility. Visiting the cottages to make sure she was safe had been a chivalrous gesture, and maybe—just maybe—she'd hoped that he would do it. But she would have expected Nero just to bark, not launch himself at Alex in attack mode. She would have a word with Ian on the subject. Injury to innocent visitors was something to be avoided. But, chivalrous or not, she reminded herself tartly, Alex's name was still Merrick. And her reaction to it was still the same as the first time she'd heard it.

On her very first day at Barclay Homes she'd found that the firm was actually a subsidiary of the Merrick Group, which had swallowed up other building firms in the area. A small outfit like her father's had never stood a chance. Sarah knew with the logical part of her that the Merrick Group had not caused his death. But the illogical, emotional side of her still held them accountable.

CHAPTER FOUR

SARAH SAW no more of Alex Merrick after their midnight encounter. But to her surprise—and disgust—she kept wondering if he'd ring, or call in again. To counteract this she worked like a demon on the last touches to the cottages while Harry painted the exteriors, and Ian moved into number two at night, rather than spoil any of Sarah's work on the show house. When she ran out of indoor jobs she repointed the waist-high walls dividing the front gardens, and when she'd finished those Charlie Baker drove her to a local nursery to choose a flowering cherry for the back courtyard of the show house, and a Japanese maple for the front. It was only sensible to go the extra mile to make the properties as attractive as possible to prospective buyers.

'Is something worrying you?' asked Harry, as he helped her plant the trees one evening.

'Yes. I'm wondering what on earth I'm going to do with myself when this lot goes up for sale.'

'What are you doing this weekend?' he asked, surprising her.

'Nothing much. Why?'

'How do you feel about barns?'

Sarah straightened, eyes gleaming. 'Are we talking barn conversion?'

He smiled as he trampled the earth in round the cherry tree. 'Could be.'

'Tell me more—' Her face fell. 'But if they're up for sale I can't do a thing about it until I sell this lot.'

'These barns are not for sale. Leastways, not yet.'

She wagged a dirty finger at him. 'Stop teasing, Harry!'

He chuckled. 'My sister's married to a farmer. When I was there for dinner last Sunday Bob told me he's had to cut back a bit, so he's got three smallish barns he doesn't use any more. He's got planning permission to do them up, but not enough cash to do it with. If you offered to buy them for development I reckon he'd jump at the chance.' He nodded in approval as Sarah's eyes sparkled. 'That's better. You've been a bit down in the mouth lately.'

'Have I? Sorry. Anyway, when could I have a look at the property?'

'I'll talk to Mavis when I get home and let you know.' He looked up as a van came up the lane. 'Here comes the nightshift.'

Sarah bent to hug Nero as he came bounding to greet her. 'Hello, my lovely boy. How are you today? Hello, you two,' she added, as the others came up the path.

'Hi, there,' said Josie, eyeing the newly planted Acer. 'Gosh, it looks better and better here every time I come. Don't you dare go lifting your leg on that tree, Nero.'

'Don't worry, Miss Carver, I'll tell him not to, and he doesn't need telling twice,' said Ian proudly.

'Of course you don't, you clever lad,' said Sarah, giving the dog a last stroke. 'Right, then, time I went home and got cleaned up. See you tomorrow, Harry.'

'I'll give you a ring later, boss.'

Sarah felt weary as she drove back, conscious of a sense of anticlimax now the cottages were ready to sell. Tomorrow three estate agents were coming at different times to view.

When the phone rang while she was eating her supper Sarah seized it eagerly. 'Harry—'

'Afraid not. It's Alex. Alex Merrick,' he added, in case she was in any doubt.

The unexpected pleasure of her reaction struck her dumb for a moment. 'Oh, hello,' she said at last.

'How are you?'

'I'm very well.'

'Glad to hear it. Are the cottages finished?'

'Just about.'

'Then let's meet to discuss the sale. Friday would be good for me.'

He still wanted them, then. 'Sorry. I can't make Friday.'

'When then?'

Never, for a Merrick, if she followed her instincts. But it would be interesting to see how high Alex would go with his offer.

'Are you still there?' he demanded.

'Yes. I could do Saturday morning.'

'Right. I'll see you at the cottages at ten.'

When the phone rang again shortly afterwards it actually was Harry, with an invitation to Sunday dinner at the farm so she could have a look round.

'How lovely! Please thank your sister for me, Harry.'

The houses passed the building inspector's final examination with flying colours, and the visits by the estate agents went equally well. They forecast figures much higher than Sarah had dared hope—the highest from one of the more exclusive agents, who assured her he'd have no trouble in shifting all six houses if she put her business in his company's hands.

But if she did Sarah knew only too well she'd lose a hefty percentage of her profit to them. But that was far preferable to selling them to a Merrick. Though she might as well meet Alex Merrick and know what figure he had in mind, if only for the pleasure of turning him down. The vice-chairman of the Merrick Group would probably beat her down mercilessly. Just let him try, she thought fiercely.

Instead of spending the evening glued to columns of figures on her laptop Sarah went early to bed that night, feeling more relaxed now the die was cast. She achieved a good night's sleep for once, and turned up at the cottages next morning full of energy for the last minute touches. She swept and dusted throughout, then buffed up the latest thing in stainless steel door furniture on each of the cottages while Harry cleaned the windows.

'But don't let on about me doing women's work,' he warned, when they went down to the Green Man at lunchtime.

Sarah zipped a finger across her lips. 'Not a word. Though you've done it miles better than this woman would have done.'

'You mean there's something you can't do, then, boss?' he teased.

'Lots of things—and cleaning windows as well as you do is way up there on the list.'

'Have you decided which agent's going to handle the sale?'

'Not yet. I'll have a chat with Oliver over the weekend and let them know on Monday.'

Close as she'd grown to Harry, Sarah felt it best to keep her meeting with Alex Merrick to herself.

She spent some time next morning over her choice of clothes for her Saturday rendezvous. Her aim was somewhere below the full-on babe outfit of an evening with Oliver but well above the scruffy look of her working day. And, most important of all, Sarah was determined to obliterate Alex's last impression of her in striped pyjamas and the dressing gown her mother had given her for her fifteenth birthday. She felt a little uneasy about seeing him again after the disaster of his encounter with Nero. But this was different; it was a business meeting, she reminded herself, though not the occasion for one of the suits she'd worn in the office. She settled for a pair of black linen trousers and a plain white shirt, and because the forecast was showery armed herself with the short black trench coat she wore for trips into Hereford. She'd treated her unruly curls to a blow-drying session for once, and tied them back with a silk scarf, then surprised her face by applying some make-up for a change, instead of just the usual smear of moisturiser—though this last came

in handy when she found she'd run out of polish for her flat
black shoes.

Sarah drove down to the cottages at nine to relieve her house-
sitters, who had tidied all their gear away and left milk for her
coffee. She thanked them warmly, and after a romp with Nero
waved them off to enjoy their weekend. Sarah went on a tour
of all six houses, then sat down in the show house to read the
paper she'd bought on the way. She skimmed through the news
items, and even did half a crossword, but at last felt too restless
to stay indoors and went outside.

After a week of sunshine and showers, the gardens in all the
cottages were looking surprisingly well established. Sarah had
time to make a thorough check on all of them before the
familiar Cherokee nosed down the lane. When Alex got out,
holding a briefcase but otherwise looking casual in jeans and
sweater, she strolled up the lane towards him.

'Good morning.' He met her halfway, smiling that smile
of his, and shook her hand. 'Congratulations. You've done a
great job here.'

'Thank you. Take yourself on a tour, if you like.'

'Come with me—please?'

'Certainly.'

This time Alex was in no hurry. He put his briefcase down
on the kitchen table, then made a thorough exploration of every
house, taking such minute notice of every feature that Sarah
was more glad than ever that she'd bought top-quality fittings—
especially when he commented on the Belfast sinks installed
in the curving, custom-built counter tops in all the kitchens.

'You've achieved a very clever balance between traditional
and modern,' he said, when they eventually returned to the
show house.

'Thank you. My aim was a country cottage with local
appeal, but which would also tempt a town buyer looking for
a weekend retreat.'

'Where did you get the vintage furniture?'

'I put the contents of my family home into storage when the house was sold. I sent for some of them last week, so I could make the show house look like a real home. At which point,' she added, 'Ian Sollers promptly moved into number two at night, to avoid any possibility of his damaging anything.'

'Not to mention any Nero might cause,' said Alex with feeling.

'Nero doesn't do damage. He's a very well-behaved dog,' said Sarah firmly. 'He was just doing his job that night.'

'You obviously love dogs!'

'I do.' Sarah shrugged. 'But even if I had room for one dogs aren't allowed at Medlar House.'

'So sell your ivory tower and move to a place where you *can* keep a pet. In your kind of job you can take a dog with you on site.'

'True,' said Sarah. 'But I don't want to move right now. I've only just got my flat into shape. Talking of property,' she added, suddenly brisk, 'would you care for some coffee while we get down to business?'

'Thank you.' Alex promptly sat at the head of kitchen table, as though chairman of the board was his rightful place.

Sarah made coffee in china cups with saucers, and carried a tray to the table. 'Only instant, I'm afraid.'

'Fine,' he said, waiting for her to sit down. 'Now, then, Miss Carver. How much do you want for the entire property?'

Sarah multiplied the highest price by six and gave him the answer.

Alex stared at her in disbelief. 'That's totally unrealistic.'

'It's the price I was advised to ask,' she assured him.

'But any other buyer would want only one cottage,' he reminded her sharply. 'If I buy the entire row you'll have to come down, Miss Carver. A long way down,' he added.

Sarah had done her homework in so much depth and so repeatedly she knew exactly how low she could go and still make the profit necessary to make her venture a success. 'I suppose I could come down a trifle.'

Alex snorted. 'You'll have to do a lot better than that!'

'Look,' she said reasonably, 'if you don't want them I'm assured I'll have no problem finding other buyers.'

He stared at her in exasperation. 'I do want them, but only at a reasonable figure.'

'You mean what the Merrick Group considers a reasonable figure!'

'Exactly. Nothing personal. It's just business.'

'I know all about the business done by the Merrick Group,' she retorted, before she could stop herself.

His eyes narrowed. 'And what, exactly, do you mean by that?' he asked, his voice dangerously quiet.

Her chin lifted. 'Merely that your group is big enough to submit tenders which put smaller companies out of business.'

Comprehension dawned in his eyes. 'You said your father was a builder—'

'He was taken over by Barclay Homes, which as you well know is a subsidiary of the Merrick Group.' Sarah wished now she'd kept her mouth shut. 'Shall we return to the matter in hand?'

'By all means,' he said curtly, and made her an offer only a little higher than the lowest possible she could accept to make a profit.

'Now *you're* being unrealistic,' she said scathingly.

The coffee cooled in the cups while they haggled, Sarah coolly resolute and Alex growing more and more exasperated as he fought a battle he'd expected to win with barely a shot fired. In the end he slapped a hand down on the table, making the cups rattle, and named a figure which was, he said very emphatically, his top offer, and Miss Carver could take it or leave it.

'Do you want your answer now?' she asked.

Alex fought for control. For God's sake, he thought furiously. He faced tougher customers than Sarah Carver every day of his working life. 'Yes,' he snapped.

She shook her head. 'I need time to think about your offer,

Mr Merrick. I quite understand,' she added, sweetly reasonable, 'if you want to back out.'

To hell with it, thought Alex. Only the prospect of unsuitable tenants on land adjoining his luxury hotel kept him from doing just that. He got to his feet and snapped his briefcase shut. 'Ring my office at nine sharp on Monday morning with your answer, or kiss the sale goodbye, Miss Carver.'

Sarah nodded briskly. She got to her feet to see him out, and followed him down the path.

'Thank you for coming. Goodbye.'

'Goodbye, Miss Carver,' he said formally, and made no further reference to the deal before driving away.

Sarah watched him go, frowning. Now she had to get through the rest of the day with nothing to do. From a practical, purely financial point of view she knew very well that she should have said yes to Alex's offer there and then. But because his name was Merrick she was not only going to turn him down, but make him wait all weekend before she did.

Sarah decided to stay on site all day, until Ian and Josie turned up in the evening. Perhaps she could persuade her young caretakers to spend the entire day here on Sunday while she was out with Harry. The weather forecast was good, and they would probably enjoy a day spent in the sun in the courtyard of number one. She'd offer to stand them a takeaway lunch as inducement. Until the cottages were sold—whoever bought them—she would need the services of her young security guards. Sarah locked up with care and drove back to the local Post Office stores to buy food, added a paperback novel to her haul, and then returned to Medlar Farm cottages for the day.

She passed some of the time with more gardening in the sunshine, though by now there was very little left to do. The shrubs looked healthy, the lawns were greening up satisfactorily, and the property as a whole was very different from the barely habitable row of houses she'd first seen with Oliver.

Sarah rang him later, to tell him about the offer she'd had from Alex Merrick.

'Splendid, darling. I'm very proud of you. Is it all signed and sealed?'

'Of course not. I haven't *accepted* the offer, Oliver.'

'You mean you didn't jump at it?' demanded Oliver in astonishment. 'My dear child, what were you thinking of?' He paused. 'I suppose if he were a rose by any other name you would have said yes to Alex right away.'

'Exactly, Oliver. How percipient of you.'

'Far be it from me to try to run your life,' he said, an edge to his voice, 'but if you're going to succeed in your line of business sentiment's a luxury you can't afford, Sarah.'

'I know, I know,' she sighed. 'Don't worry. The agents who valued the houses assure me they'll have no trouble in selling them.'

'Or in creaming off some of your profit,' Oliver reminded her.

'True. But it would be worth it,' said Sarah. 'I can't bear the thought of Merrick hotel guests living in my cottages.'

'Ah, but that's not the plan. I had a little chat with George Merrick the other night and put out some discreet feelers on the subject. Apparently young Alex intends to use the houses as retirement homes for long service employees of the Merrick Group.'

'*What?*' Sarah's eyebrows shot to her hair. 'Are you sure about that?'

'I'm merely passing on what his father told me. In confidence, by the way,' warned Oliver.

Sarah shook her head in wonder. 'I was sure Alex Merrick meant to put them to work to make money, as an annexe for his hotel.'

'I hinted as much to George. But he said that Alex, much to old Edgar's disgust, is hell-bent on philanthropy. And he makes it very plain who's in charge these days. So instead of making them pay for themselves, the cottages will house deserving ex-employees who will live in rural, rent-free bliss in your first venture into property development, Sarah. Should you sell to him, of course.'

'Well, that's a turn-up for the books,' she said, deflated, and stayed silent for a while, thinking it over.

'Are you still there, Sarah?' demanded Oliver.

'Yes. I was thinking. Much as it grieves me to say so, if what you say is true I suppose it would be a pity not to let Alex Merrick have them.'

'At the money he's offering it would be downright stupidity to turn it down, my girl. Forget about his name for once and accept his offer. As your practical father,' he added with emphasis, 'would have urged you to. And take my advice—which to anyone else is inordinately expensive—in future transactions use your head, not your heart, Sarah. And ring me on Monday to let me know what happened.'

Harry collected Sarah from Medlar House at twelve next day, in cords and a tweed jacket, and sporting a new haircut.

'You look very smart, Harry,' she told him, and dumped her rubber boots in the back of the pick-up.

'So do you,' he said, eyeing her crisp striped shirt and newly laundered jeans. 'A mighty big improvement on those overalls of yours.'

'Practically anything would be. I hope it's not putting your sister out to have an extra guest for lunch,' added Sarah.

'If you can put Mavis and Bob in the way of making a bit of money she'll be glad to do it every Sunday,' he assured her. 'They never had sons, which means paying for labour now the girls are married and can't help out any more, so things are a bit tight on the farm these days. Mind,' he added awkwardly, 'I didn't say that to influence you.'

'I know that, Harry! But it struck me yesterday that I'm going to be like a lost soul with no work to do. I do so hope the barns are a feasible proposition.'

To Sarah's intense relief they were. After introducing her to his sister and her husband, Harry kept in the background while Mavis, a smaller, jollier version of her brother, insisted on serving coffee before she let her large, amiable husband take Sarah on a tour of the barns. The meal giving out savoury aromas in the big farm kitchen would be ready in one hour exactly, Mavis informed them.

'So you'd best go too, Harry,' she said, 'and make sure Bob brings Miss Carver back here on time.'

Sarah was jubilant later, on the way home. The barns were small enough to be viable for conversion, though not to the holiday lets the Grovers had intended. Permanent dwellings were essential for Sarah to gain her necessary profit. A lane separated the barns from the main farm, and gave good access for the equipment Sarah would hire—also for the tenants who would eventually occupy the finished houses.

'What do you think, Harry?' she asked. 'If I make an offer to your brother-in-law are you game to go on working with me?'

'Wouldn't have mentioned the barns else,' he assured her. 'So you see them as a workable proposition?'

'I certainly do.' She gave him a sparkling look. 'Mr Grover told me he owns fishing rights on a short stretch of the river, too, which could appeal to male buyers. And for women who don't fish it's not far to Hereford for retail therapy.'

Harry laughed. 'You had all this worked out in your head before Mavis dished up the rhubarb crumble.'

Sarah grinned. 'I certainly did.' She sobered. 'But I can't make a firm offer until I sell the cottages. With luck I should be able to some time next week.'

'You've got someone interested in one of the cottages?'

Sarah nodded. 'I've got a possible buyer for the lot, but I haven't clinched the deal yet.'

'All six houses?' Harry took his eyes off the road for a second to look at her. 'You don't look all that pleased about it.'

Sarah smiled ruefully. 'We've been working on those cottages for quite a while now, Harry. It's a wrench to part with them.' Especially to a Merrick. 'But if the sale goes through I can start planning the new look for the barns right away. Do you think Ian and Fred will fancy helping again?'

'Try stopping them,' said Harry dryly as he drove into Medlar House. 'Now, get a good night's rest. I'll check up on the youngsters myself on the way back.'

Sarah did her best to take Harry's advice, but after a phone call from Oliver to confirm that she still intended to sell to Alex she was too wound up to sleep much—partly from excitement over the barns, but mainly because she couldn't rid herself of the idea that now, when she'd finally, reluctantly, made up her mind, Alex Merrick would say his offer had been withdrawn when she rang him to accept it.

When the sun began streaming through the shutters next morning Sarah gave up all pretence of even trying to sleep and got dressed. She let herself out of the flat, and later enjoyed her morning coffee all the more for the mile long round trip to buy a paper. She ate some toast while she caught up on the day's news, then just sat with her phone in her hand, gazing out at the sunlit garden as she waited for the appointed hour. Exactly on the stroke of nine she rang Alex Merrick's office number, and in response to Greg Harris's familiar accents told him Miss Carver wished to speak to Mr Merrick.

'I'll see if he's free,' said the young man stiffly, obviously still smarting from their previous exchange. 'Will you hold?'

'Certainly.'

'I'm putting you through,' he said a moment later, and her stomach clenched as the familiar, confident voice came on the line.

'Good morning, Miss Carver.'

'Good morning, Mr Merrick.'

'I take it you have an answer for me?'

'Yes. I accept your offer for the Medlar Farm Cottages.'

Alex was silent for so long Sarah's stomach did a nosedive. Had she been right to worry? Had he changed his mind?

'Good,' he said at last.

Her eyes kindled. Swine! He'd done that on purpose.

'I suggest,' he went on, 'that we meet here at my office at eleven tomorrow to make the exchange. Is that convenient for you?'

'Yes.'

'One of the Merrick Group lawyers will be present, and you will naturally wish to bring your own legal support.'

'Naturally,' she said crisply, praying that the solicitor Oliver had found for her would be free to accompany her into the lion's den.

'In the meantime, I'll send our chief surveyor round to the cottages today at ten to make our own official inspection—if that's convenient?' Alex said, hoping Sarah couldn't tell he was grinning from ear to ear.

'Of course,' she said coolly, and disconnected to call her solicitor and make her request.

Charles Selby, it appeared, was only too glad to accompany her, and promised to pick her up at Medlar House well before the appointed hour. Probably because she was the goddaughter of Oliver Moore QC, thought Sarah the cynic, then rang Oliver's chambers, as ordered, to give him the glad news.

'Splendid, darling,' he said, delighted. 'Congratulations. I wondered if you might change your mind at the last minute.'

'So did I,' she admitted ruefully. 'By the way, I've asked Mr Selby to go with me tomorrow, Oliver.'

'Good girl. He can brief me later. Louise and Sam would be so proud of you, Sarah. I'll drink a toast to all three of you tonight.'

Once Sarah had swallowed the lump in her throat, she rang Harry to put him in the picture.

'Well done, boss,' he said gruffly. 'But if it's not signed and sealed until tomorrow you'll need Ian again tonight.'

'I will, indeed. Then tomorrow the Merrick Group can take over. I'm driving down to the site right now to wait for their building inspector, Harry. How about celebrating with a ploughman's at the Green Man later?'

'I'm here at the cottages now,' he told her. 'Ian had to go off early this morning, so he asked me to come over.'

'Thank you, Harry, you're a star!'

'Get away with you. I'll put the kettle on.'

Sarah spent a tense morning with Harry, praying that the Merrick surveyor would find nothing wrong when he arrived to inspect the houses.

'Stop worrying,' Harry told her. 'The official building inspectors were satisfied with it, so I doubt this fellow will find anything wrong.'

'I just hope you're right,' she said fervently.

The inspector had finished by lunchtime, but to Sarah's disappointment he made no comment on the properties other than to tell her he would pass on his findings to Mr Merrick.

'I wish I knew what his findings were,' said Sarah, frustrated.

'You will, soon enough. The surveyor Bob Grover hired for his barns was just as thorough,' Harry told her.

'I'll take Mr Grover's outlay into consideration when I make my offer,' Sarah assured him. 'Though I'll need a second survey on the barns. The original intention was holiday lets, so it's vital I make sure I have the necessary permits for permanent dwellings.'

Lunch at the Green Man cheered Sarah up considerably, though Harry advised her in advance against giving the regulars her news. 'Time enough for that when the deal's gone through,' he warned.

'Don't worry, Harry. I won't breathe a word to anyone until the money's safe in my bank account.'

When they went into the bar to a chorus of greetings Sarah had to put up with some good-natured teasing about being dressed up today, instead of in her working clothes.

'You clean up pretty good, I must say,' said Fred, handing her a half of cider. 'I don't think you've met Eddy's son,' he added, indicating the man who'd just come through into the bar. 'Daniel, this is Miss Sarah Carver—the prettiest property developer in the business.'

Daniel Mason put up the flap to come round the bar and shake Sarah's hand. Unlike his stocky father, he was tall and slim, with smooth fair hair and confident blue eyes. 'I'm delighted to meet you,' he said fervently.

Sarah smiled. 'I haven't seen you in here before.'

'I'm London-based, but I'm down for a few days' break from the city grind.'

'He works in a bank,' said Harry, his tone pejorative.

Daniel laughed. 'But don't hold that against me, Miss Carver.'

'Sarah's from London,' Fred informed him. 'But she's not like any city girl you know. Brought up on a building site, weren't you, my dear?'

'Mostly,' she admitted, and smiled. 'Though I did go to school now and then.'

'Maybe you could see what's happened to our meals, Daniel,' interrupted Harry.

'Certainly,' said the son of the house, unfazed. 'Back in a minute.'

'You watch that one,' said Harry in an undertone. 'He's too clever by half.'

Since this was more or less the same comment he'd made about Alex Merrick, Sarah smiled, amused. It was obviously Harry's general attitude towards the young and successful male.

When Daniel came back with their lunches he leaned on the other side of the bar while Sarah and Harry ate, asking about the project Sarah had just finished.

'I didn't do it on my own,' she assued him. 'I had Harry's invaluable input all along, plus some from Mr Carter here, and from several other people Harry roped in along the way.'

Daniel raised an eyebrow. 'I thought you were semi-retired, Mr Sollers?'

'Miss Carver needed my help,' said Harry flatly, and turned away to talk to Fred.

'He doesn't approve of soft city-types like me,' said Daniel in an undertone, then grinned. 'Though he's best known for his disapproval of the female of the species, so how did you get him work to work for *you*?'

'Harry works *with* me,' Sarah said with emphasis. 'Lucky for me he approved of my aim to restore the cottages rather than demolish them.'

'Ah, I see! I'd like to see the result of your labours,' he added. 'May I come and marvel some time?'

'By all means.'

'Let me get you another drink.'

She shook her head, smiling. 'I must get back.'

Harry turned back to her. 'I'll drop you off, boss, then I'm going to the vicarage to measure up the window Mrs Allenby wants replaced. I'll get back to you after that and wait for Ian.'

'No need, Harry. Just run me back now and I can do the waiting. I've got nothing planned for this afternoon. I'll potter around in the gardens, then read until the night shift comes on.'

'In that case maybe I'll do a bit in my own garden.' He lifted her down from the bar stool, and Sarah said a general goodbye to everyone, including Daniel, who smiled back with a warmth so marked that Harry teased her about it as they drove back.

Sarah felt restless as she wandered through the cottages later. It would be wonderful to sell the lot, even if it were to the Merrick Group. But work on them had taken up almost her entire life until recently, and she felt a sharp pang of regret at the thought of parting with them. Idiot! As Oliver so rightly said, if she were to make any kind of success there was no room for sentiment as a property developer, even for a fledgling one like herself. Though if money had been her only aim she could have sold the cottages to a buyer who'd offered for them before she'd even left London. But the offer had been so unrealistic she'd turned it down without a second thought.

Right now she just had to get through the rest of the day, hope the building inspection had gone well, and meet with Alex in the morning. Then, once the money was in her account, she could concentrate on getting the Westhope barn development off the ground. With this cheering thought in mind, Sarah curled up with her book and settled down to wait until her young security staff arrived.

A knock on the door brought Sarah to her feet, surprised. She'd been enjoying the book, but not so much that she wouldn't have heard an approaching car. She opened the front door to find Daniel Mason smiling down at her.

'Hello, Miss Sarah Carver. I fancied a stroll, so I took you at your word.'

CHAPTER FIVE

SARAH RETURNED the smile, not sorry for company on an afternoon which was already beginning to drag. 'So you did, Daniel Mason. Come in. I'll give you the tour.'

'Thank you. Only I prefer Dan. May I call you Sarah?'

'Of course.'

'After you left,' said Dan, as she took him round, 'I was told all sorts of tall tales; how you do your own plastering and tiling and God knows what besides. That can't possibly be true?'

'Yes, all of it,' she assured him. 'But Harry saw to the basic, essential things required by the building survey. And he put in new windows and did all the finishing after I'd done my bit.'

'And no one does it better than Harry Sollers. But he's well known for preferring to work solo. So how come he agreed to work for—I mean *with*—you?'

'I asked him and he said yes.'

Dan gave her a head-to-toe scrutiny rather too personal for comfort, and grinned. 'Of course he did.'

Sarah turned to lead the way downstairs. 'This is the only one I've furnished, but otherwise the houses are all the same.'

'You've done an amazing job,' he told her. 'If they were in London they'd sell in a flash—and for a lot more than you'll get down here. I'd like to stay a while, Sarah,' he added. 'Unless you're busy?'

She could hardly say she was, since he'd spotted the open

book. 'For the first time in ages I'm not. I was reading when you came.'

'Fred told me that you've got young Ian Sollers staying here at night. What time does he get here?'

'About six, as a rule.'

'What will you do after he gets here?'

'Go home.'

'And where's home?'

'You ask a lot of questions!'

He smiled. 'It's the quickest way to get answers.'

'You could have asked around in the bar.'

Dan shook his head. 'I was pretty sure you might not like that. Though I was told,' he went on, 'that you don't socialise with the local lads. Why?'

'It seemed best to steer clear of complications in a community like this.'

'Is there a non-local man in your life?'

'Yes. My godfather. They were pretty impressed at your pub because he wined and dined me at Easthope Court recently,' she said lightly.

'Well-heeled godfather, then!'

'He's a QC, and successful, so I suppose he must be. More important from my point of view, he takes his responsibilities as godfather very seriously. He wasn't happy when I insisted on bidding for this lot,' said Sarah wryly. 'He doesn't like my flat, either.'

'At the address you didn't give me,' he reminded her.

'It's no secret. I live in Medlar House.'

'Really?' Dan grinned. 'I used to go to dances there when it was a girls' school.'

Another one! 'They were obviously popular, those dances.'

'I went to an all-male school. You bet they were popular.' His eyes gleamed reminiscently. 'Socialising with the Medlar House girls was one of the great perks of getting to the upper sixth in my place of learning, believe me.'

'Oh, I do,' she assured him.

Dan glanced at his watch. 'Damn. Time I hiked back. I promised to give Dad a hand. But I'm free later, so will you have dinner with me, Sarah? Please?'

She looked at him thoughtfully. The evening promised to be long, with the prospect of tomorrow morning's transaction hanging over her. And Dan Mason, though a lot too confident of his own charms for her taste, was here on a temporary basis, not a permanent fixture.

'I can see you weighing up the pros and cons, so just for the record I'm happily unmarried,' Dan informed her.

'Then, thank you. Dinner it is.' Why not? It would be a good way of passing what would otherwise be an interminable evening.

'Great,' said Dan, his smile a shade too smug for Sarah's taste. 'I'll pick you up at seven-thirty. Any preference for eating places?'

'Not really—as long as it's not Easthope Court.'

When Ian and Josie arrived with Nero, for their last evening as caretakers, Sarah thanked them warmly for their help.

'We'll miss coming here,' said Josie wistfully.

'If you need us somewhere else any time,' added Ian, 'you just have to say.'

'I certainly will,' Sarah promised him, and bent to give Nero a goodbye hug.

She felt quite wistful herself on the way back to the flat, but cheered up at the thought of going out. Not sure where Dan was likely to take her, she wore the tailored black linen trousers with their jacket over a cream silk camisole, and brushed her hair into a mass of loose curls. She was glad she'd taken the trouble when Dan came to collect her wearing a formal lightweight suit, topped by a look of deep approval which was highly gratifying.

'You look wonderful,' he told her.

'Thank you. Where are we going?'

'A London chef recently opened a country inn type restaurant a few miles from here. I thought you might like it.'

'Sounds perfect—' Sarah whistled as she spotted the banana-yellow Ferrari parked in the courtyard.

He patted the bonnet lovingly, then held the passenger door for her. 'This baby is my reward for slaving long hours on a City trading floor. I won't make you blush with my father's comments. Boy's toys and all that. And, as he says repeatedly, it's not even necessary. I walk to the bank from my flat.'

Sarah laughed. 'So when do you drive it?'

'At weekends.' He slanted a grin at her as he turned out into the road. 'To some country hostelry—with a charming companion on board, of course.'

'Of course. In the company I used to keep they were known as bird-pullers,' she informed him.

'Bird-pullers!' he exclaimed, laughing. 'Exactly what kind of company did you keep?'

'The kind you get on building sites.'

As Dan had promised, the inn was picturesque. Baskets of flowers hung outside a rambling low building divided inside into several small dining rooms.

'Choose anything you like from the menu. It's all first class,' Dan assured her.

He was right. But Sarah enjoyed the perfectly cooked sea bass rather more than Dan's company while she ate. Because his conversation centred on his success in his job, and the bonuses which had enabled him to buy his expensive car and his equally expensive flat, she found her attention wandering, and surfaced guiltily to hear him describing a recent holiday in St Tropez. Her brief encounters with Alex Merrick had been stormy, she thought suddenly, but a lot more interesting. Though after tomorrow there would be no more encounters. She was unlikely to see Alex again once the sale had gone through.

'That's a very thoughtful expression in those big dark eyes, Sarah Carver,' remarked Dan.

'It seems odd to think that my first venture into property development is over,' she said, smiling brightly.

'Is a second on the cards?'

'Of course. Once the sale of this one goes through.'

'Something local?'

'Yes.'

'Good.' Dan gave her his irritatingly cocky smile. 'With you around I'll be visiting the old folks more often in future.'

Sarah got up to leave. 'Around doesn't mean available.'

'I put that badly,' said Dan penitently, on their way to the car. 'Have I shot myself in the foot?'

'Not at all.'

'Then let's do this again. I'm here until the weekend. What day would suit you?'

'Sorry. I'll be too busy getting to grips with the new project.'

When they reached Medlar House Dan turned off the engine and undid his seat belt. 'I'd love a look at your flat.'

She shook her head. 'I have to be up early in the morning, so I'll just say thank you for the meal and wish you goodnight, Dan.'

He bent his head to kiss her, but Sarah put a hand on his shoulder and held him off, then released the seat belt and got out of the car. 'Thank you for dinner,' she repeated, as he followed her to the door. 'And for a pleasant evening.'

'Pleasant!' he repeated, an ugly set to his mouth. 'You really know how to cut a guy down to size.'

She smiled as she put her key in the door. 'Something you're not used to, I imagine?'

'No. Women like me as a rule.' He eyed her, baffled. 'I just wanted a kiss, for God's sake.'

'But I didn't,' said Sarah gently. 'Goodnight.'

Odd, she thought later, as she got ready for bed. Dan Mason was good-looking, and obviously clever to have done so well in his career. But he seemed to feel that his possessions were his main attributes. And he was probably right, because for some reason the thought of having him kiss her had made her skin crawl. Tonight had been a mistake. It served her right for breaking her rule about socialising with anyone local. She should have spent the evening with her book. Now she'd have to stay away from the Green Man until he'd gone back to the loft apartment he'd described in such mind-numbing detail.

Sarah woke long before the alarm went off next morning, aware the moment she opened her eyes that this was a memorable day in her life. She had no doubt about what to wear. This occasion really did call for a suit. And not just any old suit she'd worn to the office, but the raspberry-red number she'd bought for the wedding of one of her former flatmate, a couple of months before. The jacket's nipped-in waist and cleverly cut skirt were flattering, and with four-inch heels to give her height she could face up to Alex Merrick and whoever else he had on board.

By ten-thirty her solicitor hadn't arrived, and Sarah was just about to take off without him when her doorbell rang. About time, she thought irritably as she lifted the receiver.

'Sarah,' said a familiar voice. 'Are you ready?'

'*Oliver?*'

'Yes, darling. Charles Selby's here, too, so come along.'

Sarah locked her door, then rushed out into the courtyard to embrace her godfather's substantial person. 'It's so lovely to see you, but what on earth are you doing here?'

'Is that the way to greet someone who rose at the crack of dawn to fly to your side?' he asked, and kissed her cheek fondly, then looked her in the eye. 'I wanted to make sure you hadn't suffered a change of heart.'

She shook her head. 'No. I haven't.'

'Good. In that case my professional support will do no harm. Selby here has no objection.'

'Forgive my bad manners, Mr Selby.' Sarah turned to him in remorse. 'Good morning.'

The solicitor shook her hand, smiling. 'Good morning, Miss Carver. I'll follow you to the Merrick Group offices.'

Oliver ushered her into his Daimler, smiling rather smugly. 'I didn't mention my presence here beforehand, in case something unforeseen cropped up to prevent it. And my usual hotel room is free for me tonight, so I shall drive back first thing in the morning. You look utterly delightful, Sarah.'

'Good to know, because it took work,' she said with feeling, and beamed at Oliver. 'Thank you so much for coming.'

The Merrick Group offices were housed a few miles away, in a purpose-built modern building surrounded by manicured gardens. The woman at a reception desk flanked by banks of greenery smiled in enquiry at their approach.

'Miss Carver for Mr Merrick. These gentlemen are my lawyers,' Sarah said grandly.

The receptionist rang through to report their arrival, then conducted them across a gleaming expanse of parquet to a trio of lifts, and told them where to find Mr Merrick's office on the top floor.

Sarah grinned at Oliver as the lift doors closed on them. 'What cheek, talking about my lawyers! I hope you didn't mind.'

'Since both Selby and I *are* lawyers, not at all,' Oliver assured her.

'A pity you couldn't have worn your wig and gown,' she said with regret. 'Though you look impressive enough just the way you are.'

He was immaculate, as usual, his silver hair expertly styled, his superb three piece suit complete with watch chain. Mr Selby was similarly dressed, but his receding hair and smaller stature were no contest against the magnificence of Oliver Moore QC.

A tall young man in stylish spectacles greeted them as the lift doors opened on the top floor.

'Good morning, Miss Carver. I'm Gregory Harris, Mr Merrick's assistant.'

'Good morning. This is my solicitor, Mr Charles Selby, also Mr Oliver Moore QC.' A statement which impressed, just as she'd intended.

'Good morning, gentlemen. Please follow me.'

Alex got to his feet as the trio followed Greg into his office, his eyes narrowing as he saw two men flanking the vision of elegance approaching his desk. She'd pulled a fast one again, by springing not just her solicitor but a Lincoln's Inn Queen's Counsel on him as well. 'Good morning, Miss Carver—gentlemen. How nice to see you, Mr Moore.'

'You too, my boy,' said Oliver affably. 'I come *in loco parentis* for Sarah. I trust you have no objection to my presence?'

'None at all,' said Alex, equally affable.

'Good morning, Mr Merrick,' said Sarah. 'May I introduce Mr Charles Selby, my solicitor?'

There was a round of hand-shaking, including an introduction to Lewis Francis, the Merrick Group legal representative.

'Coffee?' suggested Alex.

Sarah opened her mouth to refuse, but Oliver nodded genially. 'That would be very pleasant—I had an early start.'

And, instead of getting straight down to business, as she would have preferred, Sarah was forced to make pleasant conversation with Lewis Francis while coffee was consumed, along with croissants and French pastries, which Sarah refused. She was hard put to it to swallow the coffee, let alone try chomping on a pastry. It seemed an age before Greg Harris came in to clear away and they could finally get down to business.

'Carry on then, Lewis,' said Alex at last.

Lewis Francis opened the file in front of him. 'All six houses on the property known as Medlar Farm Cottages met the standards of the building inspection, therefore the price remains as agreed privately by Miss Carver and Mr Merrick. This sum has now been paid into Miss Carver's account, if she would like to check before signing the necessary documents.'

'Ring your bank to confirm, Sarah,' said Oliver casually.

Sarah took out her phone to do so, and felt a surge of pure adrenaline as she heard the new total. 'Yes,' she said quietly. 'It's there.'

Eventually, when the contracts held the necessary signatures, and all was legally finalised even to Oliver's satisfaction, instead of the expected relief Sarah felt an overpowering sense of anticlimax.

'Congratulations, Miss Carver,' Alex said, holding her hand a fraction longer than necessary after shaking it.

'Thank you.'

'May I ask if you have another project in mind?'

'I do, yes.'

'Locally?'

'Yes.'

'How interesting.' He smiled his crooked smile, his eyes holding hers. 'I wish you every success with it.'

'Splendid,' said Oliver, watching the exchange like a hawk. 'I suggest I take everyone to lunch to celebrate.'

Due to other appointments, both solicitors regretfully declined, but Alex thanked Oliver warmly. 'I know the very place.'

'If you mean Easthope Court, Alex, I'd rather something more conventional at lunchtime,' warned Oliver.

'I promise you'll like the place I have in mind, sir,' Alex assured him. 'And, to let us enjoy a celebratory glass of wine with our lunch, one of the company cars will take us there.'

Oliver sat up front with the driver on the journey, leaving Sarah alone in the back of the limousine with Alex.

'You look dauntingly elegant today,' he remarked in an undertone.

Sarah shot him a surprised look. 'If that's a compliment, thank you.'

'You should always wear that colour.'

'Not a good choice for a building site.'

'Though as a matter of interest,' he added casually, as though discussing the weather, 'you look equally appealing in those overalls of yours.'

Sarah swallowed, her eyes fixed on the passing scenery. 'Practical in my line of work.'

'You didn't tell me your godfather was joining us today.'

'I didn't know. He turned up this morning as a surprise.'

He slanted a narrow look at her. 'When I saw we had the benefit of Queen's Counsel at the meeting I assumed you didn't trust me.'

'Not at all,' she returned. 'Mr Selby's presence was quite enough. Having Oliver along was just a bonus. It was good to have the support of a relative.'

'I thought he was just your godfather?'

She shook her head. 'He's also my mother's cousin, and they were as close as brother and sister, so Oliver's been in my life since I was born. He's a very hands-on godfather. Though he disapproves of my way of earning my living. When you first saw us at Easthope Court that night he was doing his best to persuade me to take a secretarial job in his chambers.'

Alex grinned broadly. 'How did you react to that?'

'Predictably.' Sarah sighed. 'I keep telling him he shouldn't worry so much about me.'

'Then I assume you didn't mention your idea of acting as your own security guard?'

Sarah shook her head vigorously, and laid a finger on her lips. 'Don't rat on me. Please!'

Chatting to Alex had been so unexpectedly easy for once that she hadn't noticed where they were heading, until the car turned into the forecourt of the inn Dan Mason had taken her to the night before.

'This looks very inviting,' said Oliver in approval as Alex helped Sarah out. 'I wonder if they do a good steak here.'

'They certainly do,' Alex assured him, then smiled as the chef himself appeared to welcome them. 'Hi, Stephen.'

'Back again, Alex? I must be getting something right.'

'We want something special today, my friend. It's a celebration.'

Stephen Hicks shot an appreciative look at Sarah. 'What kind?'

'Business deal. Let me introduce you…'

They were settled at their table before Sarah finally managed to say her piece. 'Oddly enough,' she said to Oliver, 'I had a meal here last night.'

'Did you, darling?' He looked at Alex, who shook his head regretfully.

'Not with me, alas.'

'Dan Mason from the Green Man brought me,' said Sarah, irritated to feel her colour rise.

Alex's mouth turned down. 'Son of the landlord and our local *wunderkind*. He's quite a lad, our Daniel.'

'With women?' said Oliver sharply.

'Probably,' Alex agreed. 'But actually I meant that he's a prodigy in the brain department. We went to the same school, but my interests were cricket and rugby while Dan sailed through every exam and took a first in Maths at Oxford.'

'But you went to Cambridge. Your father was very proud of that,' observed Oliver.

Alex smiled. 'My academic results weren't that spectacular.'

'But of course they didn't matter,' said Sarah. 'You had a tailor-made career waiting for you.'

His smile faded. 'Yes,' he agreed shortly.

'Now, then,' said Oliver quickly, perusing the menu. 'Let's get down to the serious business of food. What did you have last night, Sarah?'

'Sea bass,' she said, smiling at him. 'It was wonderful.'

'Stephen does an excellent rib-eye steak with oyster sauce, sir,' said Alex, and looked at Sarah. 'I had that last night.'

'You were here?' she said, startled.

'Yes. But, having interrupted your lunch once before at the Green Man, it seemed best not to incur your wrath by intruding on your dinner with Dan.'

'I'm sure Sarah wouldn't have minded in the slightest,' said Oliver, breaking the awkward little silence, and smiled as a waitress appeared to take their order. 'Have you two decided?'

The lunch party was a success, rather to Sarah's surprise, though looking back on it she thought that might have owed something to the champagne Alex ordered. Whether it was the champagne or the sheer relief of having the sale signed and settled, Sarah found herself enjoying the meal far more than the one she'd shared with Dan Mason the night before. After only a few minutes of Dan's achievements and possessions she'd been bored. Whereas every time she was in Alex Merrick's vicinity she might feel tense, as though she were balancing on a tightrope, but never for an instant bored. After toasts had been drunk to the successful business of the morning, she settled down to savour her triumph along with the award-winning food.

'So, Sarah, what do you have in mind for your next venture?' asked Alex as he refilled her glass.

'Barn conversion.'

'In this locality?'

'Yes.'

'I haven't heard of anything,' he said, surprised.

'You wouldn't have done. I heard of it through a friend.'

'Sarah seems to have established herself very successfully in the community,' remarked Oliver with satisfaction, and raised his glass again. 'To my clever goddaughter.'

'To Sarah,' said Alex, following suit.

Sarah smiled wryly. 'Not so long ago, Oliver, you were trying to persuade me to work in your chambers.'

'I concede my mistake,' he said nobly. 'I was worried about you, I freely admit, but I'm more than happy to be proved wrong.'

Alex eyed her challengingly. 'I'd still like to know how you stole a march on me over the cottages, Sarah. Our original offer was supposed to include them when we bought the Medlar Farm site, but they slipped through some red tape keyhole and went up for separate auction. And a sealed bid at that. So how did you do it?'

'I received very good advice,' she said demurely.

'That was your doing, sir?' asked Alex.

Oliver shook his head. 'Nothing to do with me, dear boy. I merely enlisted some professional advice to make sure the houses were worth buying, and then advised Sarah to bid slightly over the odds. It obviously worked.'

'Are you using the same strategy this time, Sarah?' asked Alex.

'Unnecessary. There's no auction involved.'

'More than one barn, darling?' asked Oliver

'Three, in fact.' She smiled at Alex. 'But I'd rather not give details in present company.'

Alex looked at her levelly. 'Relax, Sarah. The Medlar Farm cottages were a one-off deal because they adjoin the hotel development. Normally we don't deal in property on such a small scale.'

'Which certainly puts me in my place,' she said lightly. 'I wonder if they have more of the hazelnut parfait I had last night?'

When they arrived back at the Merrick building Alex told his chauffeur to drive Oliver back in the Daimler.

'I took it for granted you wouldn't care to drive yourself, sir,' he said, smiling.

'No, indeed. Wouldn't do for a man in my line to risk it after that extra brandy. Thank you, my boy,' said Oliver, shaking his hand. 'Very civil of you. We can drop Sarah off at her place on the way.'

Alex shook hands very formally with Sarah, before helping her into Oliver's car. 'Good luck with the new project.'

'Thank you.' She racked her brains to find something appropriate to say to mark the occasion, but in the end, feeling unexpectedly forlorn, merely smiled back at Alex as the car drew away.

CHAPTER SIX

OLIVER ASKED the driver to wait for a few minutes when they arrived at Medlar House, and followed Sarah into her flat. 'So, then, Sarah. How do you feel after your first success in the property world?'

'A bit flat,' she confessed. 'And a bit headachy, too, after two glasses of champagne at this time of day. Not,' she added with a grin, 'that it normally features in my life at *any* time of day.'

'You can well afford the odd bottle now, darling, if you fancy it,' he reminded her, then smiled lovingly. 'Sit down, darling. There's something I want to say.'

Sarah eyed him in trepidation as she went to her window-seat. 'Is something wrong, Oliver?'

'Not wrong, exactly.' He stood looking out at the view. 'I need to put something right. Your father asked me to keep it from you, but I think it's time you knew that he was asked to stay on as manager of SC Construction when the Merrick Group bought it from him.'

Sarah stared at him for a moment, then shook her head vehemently. 'That's not true. He would have told me—'

'Sam didn't tell you because he just didn't want the job. As long as you had security from the sale of the company, plus the value of the house, he was satisfied. He asked me to take care of you. Not that he needed to ask.' Oliver bent to take her hand. 'Sam's heart was giving out on him. Unknown to me, or obviously to you, he'd been taking medication for years, but when he told me he had very little time left, my darling—'

'But why didn't he tell *me*?' Sarah jumped to her feet. 'He shouldn't have kept it from me. If I'd known I would have taken more care of him.'

'You couldn't have taken better care of him than you did, Sarah.' Oliver took her in his arms and held her gently for a moment or two, then let her go and turned her face up to his. 'Sam made me promise not to tell you, but I have no compunction in breaking that promise because I believe you deserve the truth. Don't be sad. Enjoy your triumph, darling.'

Sarah nodded dumbly as she blinked tears away.

'Good girl.' Oliver bent to kiss her cheek. 'Now, I'd better not keep Alex's driver waiting any longer. Keep me in the picture with the barn conversion scheme.'

'Of course.' She hugged him hard. 'Thank you so much for coming today.'

'Least I could do, dear child.' He patted her back. 'And now I shall repair to my hotel room and sleep off the effects of lunch, before attacking the brief I brought with me.'

Sarah released him, looking at him steadily. 'And thank you for telling me the truth, Oliver.'

He smiled ruefully. 'I just hope I haven't ruined your day.'

'No. I'm glad I know. I also know how busy you are. It was wonderful to have your support today. Goodbye, Oliver. I'll ring you.'

Sarah put her suit away, washed her face, then took a long bath, her brain revolving in circles as it tried to come to terms with Oliver's revelation. At least, she thought eventually, it scotched any last remnants of guilt she'd felt about selling out to the Merrick Group. But when she'd flung her accusation at Alex Merrick why hadn't *he* told her the truth? But if he had would she have believed him? Probably not, she decided honestly. Believing anything good of the Merricks would have been difficult after years of looking on them as the villains of her particular piece. Yet in some ways she was relieved, because no matter how much she'd tried not to she liked Alex. And she was pretty sure her father would have liked him just as much as Oliver did.

Later, feeling a lot better with that thought in mind, she decided to pass the rest of the day doing girl things for once. As a start she gave her feet a rare pedicure, painting her toenails candy-pink, and then neatened her sorely tried fingernails with an emery board and painted them to match. Afterwards, with an eye on the sunlight filtering through the blinds, she hunted out a white halter top and a thin rose-print cotton skirt she hardly ever wore. Then, armed with a cup of strong coffee to chase away the last lingering effects of the champagne, she made for her usual perch on the windowseat to ring Harry.

'Hi, it's Sarah. Guess what? I've sold the entire row of cottages to the Merrick Group, so Westhope Farm here we come! Will your brother-in-law be available if we pop over there in the morning?'

Harry gave a hoot of laughter. 'No doubt about that, boss. Congratulations! What time shall I pick you up?'

Sarah smiled as she disconnected. The people who thought of Harry Sollers as a gruff old curmudgeon didn't know him as well as she did. Dedicated bachelor he might be, but he felt paternal where she was concerned. And she was grateful for it. But right now she needed to switch off for a while. Tomorrow, she promised herself, stretching, she would think about permits and building inspections and checks on footings and the usual run-up to a job. But tonight she would just chill for a while, savour her first success while she took a walk in the early evening sun round the Medlar House grounds. Afterwards she would watch something mindless on television, or read her book, or even just sit and do nothing at all for once in her life.

Heartily sick of the entire programme by late evening, Sarah was delighted to hear her phone ring—even when she found her caller was Alex Merrick. Or maybe, she decided honestly, *because* it was Alex Merrick.

'If you're not busy,' he said, after the formalities were over, 'I'd like a word.'

'By all means.' She laughed a little. 'Please don't say you want your money back.'

'Not much chance of that, with your heavy legal guns trained on this morning's proceedings! I'll be with you in a few minutes,' he added, surprising her.

'Oh—right.' Sarah's eyebrows rose as she snapped her phone shut. She'd assumed he meant a word on the phone. Now their business dealings were over the last thing she'd expected was another visit from Alex Merrick.

A quick phone call was exactly what Alex had intended, but at the sound of Sarah's voice he'd felt a sudden urge to see her, talk to her face to face. Now the deal was sorted, there was no reason why they couldn't be friends. He was thoughtful as he took the road for Medlar House. The idea of Sarah Carver as a friend was actually very appealing. His old schoolfriends, and others of both sexes he'd made in his Cambridge days, were either married or working in all four corners of the globe. Except for Stephen Hicks. And none of them had as much in common with him as Sarah from a career point of view.

When he pressed her bell Sarah buzzed him in and stood barefoot at her open door. She smiled as Alex crossed the hall towards her, unaware that she was backlit by the light streaming through her thin skirt, giving him an X-ray view of legs and curving hips that struck him dumb. 'Hi. Do come in.'

'Thank you for seeing me,' he said, clearing his throat. 'I thought you might be out celebrating.'

'Not twice in one day,' she assured him as she closed the door. 'Besides, Oliver wouldn't have risked driving here again.'

'You could have been celebrating with someone other than your godfather.' Like Dan Mason, perish the thought.

'True, but as you see I'm not, so can I offer you a glass of wine?'

Alex eyed her hopefully. 'I don't suppose you'd have a beer?'

'Sorry. The only other thing on offer is coffee.'

'Good as yours is, I'll take the wine on an evening like this.' He badly needed something to lubricate the mouth that had dried at the sight of her in silhouette. 'But only if you'll join me.'

Knowing she could depend on the quality of the wine Oliver sometimes brought her to keep in her fridge, Sarah filled two of her mother's best glasses and handed one to Alex. 'Do sit down,' she invited.

He waited for her to take her usual perch on the window-seat, then sat on the sofa, trying not to stare at her pink toenails. Her untidy curls framed a face bare of even lipstick, he noted with amusement. As usual she'd made no attempt to tidy herself up to meet him. But, polished and perfect though she'd been for their meeting this morning, he liked the barefoot dishevelled look far more. So much more it was taking all his will-power to stay on the sofa instead of snatching her up in his arms to kiss her senseless. Whoa! Where had that come from? He swallowed some wine hastily. The first step, Merrick, is to get her used to the idea of you as a friend.

Sarah waited patiently for Alex to speak. His lean, clever face looked very brown in the light above his open white collar, and for once she considered him solely on the merit of his looks—which, she had to admit, were considerable. She had always been attracted to brains rather than muscles, but Alex had both. He had a degree, so he obviously had brains, and if the muscles came from playing cricket rather than hard, physical work, at least he had some.

'What did you want to discuss?' she asked, after an interval where he seemed inclined just to sit and look at her rather than talk.

With effort, Alex removed his gaze from the hair curling on her bare shoulders. 'Have you forgotten about the furniture, Sarah?'

Not Miss Carver any more, then. She frowned. 'What furniture?'

'The first Medlar Farm cottage in the row is full of your belongings,' he reminded her.

Sarah's eyes widened. 'Good heavens!' She shook her head in disbelief. 'I can't believe I'd forgotten that. No more champagne at lunchtime for me!'

He shook his head. 'You were merely enjoying your first triumph too much to remember.'

'Which is pretty stupid of me, because it's my mother's furniture!'

'You think of it as hers rather than belonging to both your parents?' Alex gave her the benefit of his crooked smile. 'Forgive my curiosity.'

Sarah was pretty sure most people forgave him anything when he smiled like that. But she wasn't most people. 'I was speaking literally. It actually *was* my mother's. She inherited it from her parents, along with the house—but I mustn't bore you with my life history.'

'It wouldn't bore me—quite the opposite. I'd really like to hear it. Unless you find it painful to talk about your parents?' he added quickly.

To her surprise, she found she wanted to talk about them. 'My mother was a landscape gardener. She was working in the grounds of a big property when my father arrived with his crew to do restoration work on the house. One look and that was it— for both of them.' Sarah smiled wryly. 'Dad said her parents were not exactly thrilled when their only child told them she'd fallen in love with a builder brought up in a children's home. But when they met him they liked him. So much so that eventually they suggested he moved into their home with Louise after their marriage, instead of taking her away from it. Dad told me that he was only too happy to be part of a family at last, and from then on he did all the maintenance work on their sizeable North London home as a way of showing his gratitude.'

'As a son-in-law he was a valuable asset, then?'

'In every way,' Sarah agreed. 'He helped Mother care for her parents as they got older and frailer. How about you?' she added. 'I heard that your father's based in London these days?'

Alex nodded soberly, and drank some of his wine. 'Did your source tell you he'd remarried?'

'No. My "source", as you put it, is Harry Sollers. He's not big on gossip. He just gave me the bare bones of the Merrick success story.'

Alex smiled wryly. 'Then he must have mentioned Edgar, my grandfather, scrap baron extraordinaire. The old boy's a bit of a legend in this part of the world.'

'For turning scrap metal into gold?'

'That's not far off the truth. He started from nothing, which is hard to believe when you think of the group's present level of expansion.'

'Is he still alive?'

'God, yes. In his late eighties and still alive and kicking. My aunt—a saint by any standards—lives with him, and does her best to care for the cantankerous old devil.' Alex grinned at the look on Sarah's face. 'Don't look so shocked. I say exactly the same to his face.'

'If your father has remarried, did you lose your mother when you were young, like me?' she asked with sympathy.

He was silent for a moment. 'I suppose you could say that,' he said at last. 'After I graduated she divorced my father and bought a house near her sister in Warwickshire.'

'Alex, I'm so *sorry*. I wouldn't have asked if I'd known,' Sarah said remorsefully.

'At least it shocked you into calling me Alex at last.'

'I could hardly do that while you were still addressing me as Miss Carver.'

'I make it a rule never to mix business with pleasure. But,' he said, holding her eyes, 'we concluded the business part this morning, Sarah.'

'So we did.' She took his empty glass. 'Let me give you a refill. Or I could make you some coffee.'

'Does that mean you'd like me to stay awhile?'

She nodded. 'I was feeling a bit lost until you came. I've been so busy lately it was strange to have time on my hands.'

'You could have contacted Dan Mason to keep you company.'

'No, I couldn't,' she said flatly.

'Why not? You were having a good time with him last night.'

She glared at him. 'You were *watching* me?'

Alex's eyes glittered coldly. 'From where I was sitting I had no option. You didn't notice me when you arrived, but Danny boy did. He deliberately seated you with your back towards me, so he could catch my eye now and again to make sure I noticed what fun you were having together.'

'Why would he do that?' she said, astonished. 'Besides, just between you and me, it wasn't much fun. In fact it was boring. Whereas—' She stopped dead.

'Whereas?' he repeated suavely.

'I never feel bored with you,' she said, and flushed, eyeing him so warily he almost threw the 'good friends' idea to the wind and snatched her up in his arms.

'Then now we've got the business deal out of the way, there's no reason why we can't be friends.' He smiled persuasively. 'We have a lot in common, Sarah. We property developers should stick together. Which is why I offered you the services of our security men. Your crack-brained idea of sleeping at the cottages worried the hell out of me.'

'Did it?' she said, surprised.

He nodded grimly. 'I would have hated the thought of anyone at risk down there on their own, but in your case it was even worse.'

'Why? Because I'm a girl?'

'And a small one, at that.' Alex looked her in the eye. 'One I'd like to have for a friend.'

Sarah looked back very steadily. The idea of Alex as a friend appealed to her more strongly than she wanted him to know. The only friends she had in this part of the world were on the elderly side. Besides, since he was in the same line of business, broadly speaking, a friend like Alex Merrick could be very useful.

Alex eyed her curiously, aware that she was debating with herself. 'While you're thinking it over, enlighten me. Why did you say yes to dinner with Dan Mason when you always refused me? Because I'm one of the local lads you won't socialise with? Dan's local too,' he reminded her.

She shrugged. 'Only temporarily. Besides, if you rule out mixing business with pleasure you shouldn't have been asking me out in the first place.'

'For you I broke my rule. Gladly.' His eyes held hers. 'But where you're concerned, Sarah Carver, I had other cards stacked against me. Not only am I local, my name is Merrick!'

They gazed at each other in silence for a long interval. 'Today,' said Sarah slowly, 'I found out I've been wrong about that. Oliver told me my father was offered a job as manager when his firm was taken over.'

Alex nodded. 'It's group policy in those circumstances.'

'Why didn't you put me right about it?'

'Would you have believed me?'

Sarah flushed, and turned away from the bright, searching eyes. 'Probably not. But I feel pretty terrible about it now.'

'Why did Mr Moore tell you the truth today—of all days?'

Sarah raised her eyes to his. 'He obviously thought it was time I stopped gunning for you. He likes you, Alex.'

'I'm glad.' He smiled. 'But I'd be far happier if I thought *you* liked me too, Sarah.'

'I do,' she said simply.

Alex felt a surge of triumph so intense it took him by surprise. 'Good.'

He held out his hand. 'Shall we shake on it?'

'Shake on what, exactly?'

'Our friendship,' he told her, his smile even more crooked than usual.

Sarah smiled back and took the proffered hand, startled

by the frisson of response to the brief contact. 'Done,' she said lightly.

'Enlighten me, Sarah. The moment I introduced myself at Easthope Court that night you turned to ice. I know the reason now, yet you seemed to notice me earlier on. Why?'

'Your hair.'

Alex stared at her blankly. 'It's nothing out of the ordinary.'

'Ah, but the other men at your table were bald, or getting that way, so your luxuriant locks caught my eye,' she informed him, eyes sparkling. 'You were years younger than most of the men in the place, too.'

'It's an expensive restaurant. So unless they're footballers or hedge fund managers the male clientele tends to be elderly.' His lips twitched. 'Unlike their companions.'

'Which is why you took it for granted I was Oliver's current trophy!'

'A natural mistake.'

'You made your opinion so insultingly clear I wanted to punch you in the nose,' she informed him.

'You can now, if you like,' he offered.

She grinned. 'Not in cold blood.'

The last way he could describe his own. Alex itched to run his tongue over her unpainted lips, just to see if they tasted as good as they looked. He raised his glass instead. 'So shall we drink to an end to hostilities?'

She thought it over and raised her glass, nodding. 'I like the idea of being friends, Alex Merrick—'

'For God's sake just say Alex,' he said irritably.

'If we're going to be friends, Alex *Merrick*,' she snapped, ignoring his groan as she hurled his surname at him like a missile, 'we get things clear from the start. You don't give me orders.'

'God knows why I worried about you,' he said, shaking his head. 'You may be small, but you're damned vicious.' He held out his hand. 'Now, sit down and be nice.'

Sarah smiled unwillingly. 'I'll make some coffee first.'

'An offer I can't refuse. You make great coffee. One of several indelible memories from the night I met Nero!' He got to his feet to follow her to the narrow, high-ceilinged kitchen, but she held up her hand.

'You can hover in the doorway if you like, but there's only room for me in here.'

Alex leaned against the doorjamb, admiring the economy of her movements in the narrow space. 'I wanted you as a friend from the first, incidentally, before you even put me right about your relationship with Oliver.'

'You mean you saw me in my dirty overalls in the pub and wanted me for a chum?' she mocked, her eyes wide when she turned round to see Alex nodding.

'More or less,' he said lightly, accepting the mug she gave him. 'Now, this isn't an order, but a friendly word of advice. Say no to future cosy dinners with Dan Mason.'

'Why? Just because you don't like him?'

Alex shrugged. 'I disapprove of him rather than dislike him, I suppose. We went to the same school, but I belonged to a different set.'

'Because you came from a wealthier family?' Sarah couldn't help asking.

Alex held on to his temper with both hands, and sat down on the sofa, patting the place beside him. 'Do you think that one day you might try to think the best of me rather than the worst? I *meant* that I was good at most kinds of sport, and had to work a bit to pass exams, whereas Dan flew through exams but was a total duffer at any sport at all. So we didn't mix.'

'Sorry,' she said penitently, and sat down. 'But why do you disapprove of him?'

'Because, although Ed and Betty Mason are the salt of the earth, and he's their pride and joy, rumour has it that he rarely drives down from London in his Ferrari to see them. And when he does he never stays long.'

'Do you disapprove of his car, too, then?' she asked, smiling.

He looked down his nose. 'Only the colour.'

Sarah laughed, then looked at him thoughtfully. 'Do you see much of your family?'

Alex shrugged. 'I check on my grandfather most days, just to make sure he's still there. He thinks he's immortal, but in the natural way of things even he can't live for ever.'

'How about your father?'

'I see him when I visit the London office.'

Sarah slanted a glance at him. 'So you're filial and Dan is not. Is that your only objection?'

'No.' He thought it over. 'I just don't like him. I never have. He's the type who measures success by the material possessions it buys him.'

'But he's entitled if he's worked hard for them, surely?'

Alex turned to look at her. 'I've worked hard, too. Damned hard. I still do. Just because I was born a Merrick it doesn't mean I had everything handed to me on a plate. Once I was old enough I slogged on building sites or in warehouses every school holiday and university vacation unless I was on a cricket tour. And I always got landed with the hardest, dirtiest jobs.' He stretched out an arm and flexed it. 'I didn't get these muscles behind a desk, Sarah. And there was no gap year for yours truly, either. I went straight from Cambridge into the firm. Not,' he added emphatically, 'that I minded. It was always what I wanted to do. Still is.'

'I can relate to that. Because I'm doing exactly what I've always wanted to do,' said Sarah. 'And my school holidays were spent on building sites, too. But not because I was made to. Dad couldn't keep me away.'

Alex couldn't help touching her bare arm. 'But your muscles are a lot prettier than mine.' He raised her hand to his lips, and on impulse kissed each finger. 'What's wrong?' he asked, as he felt her tense.

'You say you want to be friends, but you behave more like a lover. Or at least,' she added with scrupulous honesty, 'how

I imagine a lover would behave.' None of the boyfriends she'd had in the past had practised subtlety as foreplay.

'You're a very appealing female, Sarah Carver, and I'm your average male, so I want to touch.' Need to—even crave to, more like it. He batted the thought away and smiled down at her. 'But all I ask for is friendship. Unless you're seized with overpowering lust for my body and sweep me off to bed right now, of course.'

Sarah's gurgle of laughter entranced him. 'How would I drag you up there?'

'And, having got me there, would the platform be up to it if I threw you down on the bed?' he said, grinning.

'Are you criticising my carpentry, Alex?'

He shook his head vigorously. 'I wouldn't dare.'

'Besides, I thought I was the one throwing you on the bed.'

'Let's change the subject,' he said, clapping a hand to his heart, 'before I get out of hand and risk our friendship before we even get it off the ground.'

'OK,' she said cheerfully. 'What shall we talk about?'

Alex took her hand again, instead of putting his arm round her as he badly wanted to. 'Tell me what Miss Property Developer has in mind for her next project. Purely as a friend,' he added piously, 'not as competition.'

'Oh, I know that. You made it clear that my kind of project is just chicken feed in the eyes of the Merrick Group,' she reminded him tartly.

'Only to set your mind at rest,' he assured her. 'So talk to me, Sarah. I'm interested.'

'Curious, you mean!' she said, laughing, secretly only too happy to talk at length about her plans for the barns at Westhope Farm.

Alex listened intently, made constructive comments and suggestions, and even offered Sarah any help she might need.

'For free?'

'Of course,' he assured her. 'What else are friends for?'

It was late before Alex forced himself to his feet. 'It's time we were both in bed.' He eyed the sleeping platform and grinned. 'But for various reasons not, alas, together.' He took her hand and kissed her cheek. 'Now we've agreed to be friends, let's have dinner tomorrow night.'

Sarah had to admire his style. 'Why not? Where?'

'You'll probably laugh,' he said, the crooked smile much in evidence.

'Try me.'

'I'd like to go back to Stephen's place and have you all to myself this time, without Oliver Moore watching me like a hawk, or Dan smirking at me. Just you and me, Sarah. Two friends enjoying a meal together.'

In bed later, Sarah tossed and turned, unable to sleep. Her first business triumph would have been enough to keep her awake, but Alex's visit was adding to her insomnia. His visit had been such a welcome interruption to her evening it was hard, now, to believe she'd ever looked on him as the enemy. It would be good, more than good, to have him as a friend. In fact, given the slightest encouragement, she would look on him as a lot more than just a friend— She shot upright as her phone rang.

'Hi,' said Alex.

Sarah subsided against her pillows. 'Hi.'

'Did I wake you?'

'No.'

'The glow of your first success keeping you awake?'

'That's only part of it.'

'So what else is on your mind?'

'I've realised I've agreed to a truce with the enemy,' she said bluntly.

Alex's laugh sent a tingle down her spine. 'Only I'm not the enemy any more, Sarah, am I?'

'No,' she admitted, after a pause. 'Which is pretty hard to believe.'

'I'll help you work on that tomorrow. Now, I'll tell you why I rang.'

'Not just to say goodnight?'

'That too. But I was on my way to bed before I remembered we still haven't settled about what to do with your furniture, Sarah.'

She groaned. 'Not again! I got so carried away with all my talk about barn conversions the furniture went out of my head. I'll contact my storage people and ask them to fetch it.'

'Why not store it down here? You can use one of our container units for a very reasonable fee—much cheaper than in London.'

'Oliver paid for the storage. My only outlay was getting it transported down here.'

'Where it might as well stay, ready to use in future when the barns are finished.'

'That depends on what you mean by a reasonable fee!'

'We'll discuss it tomorrow over dinner. Goodnight.'

'Goodnight.' Sarah closed her phone, then went straight to sleep with a smile on her face.

CHAPTER SEVEN

SARAH WOKE next morning to a feeling of well being. And this, she admitted, was not just due to her success on the first rung of the property ladder. Her new relationship with Alex was the icing on the cake—*and* the cherry on top. Even if he was a Merrick. He was a clever lad all round, she conceded, as she got ready for her trip with Harry. Alex was obviously brilliant at his job, or he wouldn't be vice-chairman of the Merrick Group at his age. Though apparently being born a Merrick wasn't enough to make it automatic. But it surprised her that he'd worked through most of his vacations. She'd imagined him sunning himself in the Bahamas or skiing in Gstaad, certainly not slogging away on building sites.

When Harry arrived to collect her his eyes were twinkling in his weatherbeaten face. 'Who's a clever girl, then?' he said as she got up beside him.

'I am,' said Sarah, beaming. 'But then, look what wonderful help I had!'

'Get away with you. By the way, Mavis is sorry she can't cook lunch today; she was called away late last night. My niece went into labour about midnight.'

'Oh, wow! Panic stations, then. Didn't Grandpa want to go too?'

Harry guffawed. 'Bob drove Mavis to the hospital, then cleared off back home, glad to keep well out of it.'

Sarah rolled her eyes. 'Don't tell me—women's work!'

'Yes, thank God. Bob can help birth a calf without turning a hair, but he was in a right old state about Rosemary when he rang me this morning.'

'If he's not up to it this morning we can do this another day, Harry.'

Harry shook his head. 'Bob's made up because you're thinking of buying, don't you worry. But I told him not to get his hopes up until we take another good look at the barns. Then afterwards I'll buy you a pasty in the Green Man to celebrate.' He shot her a glance. 'I thought you might like to give Fred the news.'

Sarah hadn't the heart to say no, Dan Mason or not. 'Of course. Everyone else, too,' she assured him.

When they got to Westhope Farm Bob Grover was grinning from ear to ear as he came to meet them. 'Good morning both—great news. My grandson arrived half an hour ago, and Rosemary's fine!'

Sarah and Harry opted for coffee rather than alcohol to wet the baby's head, then went on a tour of inspection with the jubilant grandfather. This time Sarah examined every inch of each building, and climbed up ladders into haylofts and down again with a speed and agility the men watched with respect. A surveyor was necessary for the official inspection, but Sarah took sets of measurements inside and out for her own personal record, including the space between each barn and its neighbour.

'You can get a good garden for each one,' Harry told her, casting a practised eye over the land available. 'It's a plus that they're offset from each other. Gives a bit of privacy.'

'I know the buildings are sound from the inspection I had done,' said Bob, not without pride. 'I'll give you a copy of the report.'

'Thank you, Mr Grover, that's a big help.' Sarah smiled at him in reassurance. 'A second one is purely to make sure of permission for permanent homes.'

Eventually Sarah confirmed that she would make a sound offer once she received a report from the building surveyor.

'This is a bigger job all round,' said Harry as they drove back.

'I know. But my dad did quite a few barn conversions at one time. I know the drill. As long as the main structures are sound on the ones at Westhope I don't see any problem. Are you in for the long haul, Harry?'

'Yes, boss,' he said, and shot her a glance. 'But this time we'll probably need more help, so I hope you got a good price for those cottages.'

Sarah nodded happily. 'It took some pretty fierce bargaining, but I did all right, Harry.'

'I don't doubt it,' he said, chuckling.

Secretly, Sarah would have preferred to go straight home. With the prospect of dinner with Alex later she didn't fancy a pasty for once. She fancied a run in with Dan Mason even less, and felt relieved when there was no sign of him when they got to the Green Man. But after she'd managed to convince Harry a sandwich was all she wanted, it was Dan who brought it through for her.

'You still here, then, Daniel?' said Harry. 'You don't usually stay so long.'

'I had my reasons,' he said, smiling pointedly at Sarah. 'And how are you today?'

'She's on top form,' said Harry, and beckoned Fred to join them. 'She sold all the cottages in one go yesterday.'

Fred beamed, and gave Sarah a smacking kiss on her cheek. 'Congratulations. Did you hear that, Charlie?'

Charlie Baker came to add his congratulations, and for a while Sarah was surrounded by well wishers wanting to buy her drinks she promised to accept next time.

When Harry was temporarily engrossed in conversation with Fred, Dan leaned closer to Sarah.

'Lucky lady,' he said in an undertone.

'Hard work, not luck,' she said dismissively.

'Something I know a lot about,' he reminded her, and smiled conspiratorially. 'So let's celebrate over dinner tonight.'

'Sorry. I can't.'

The smile vanished. 'Can't or won't?' he demanded, in a tone she didn't care for. 'I take it you've got a better offer?'

Sarah began to feel uncomfortable as eyes turned in their direction.

'Pity you didn't have a pasty, Sarah,' interrupted Harry. 'Your mother's excelled herself today, Daniel.'

'I'll have one next week,' she promised, and finished her cider.

'By then you'll be back in London, I expect, Daniel?' said Fred.

Dan nodded coolly. 'That's right, Mr Carter. It's back to the grind for me on Monday.'

Fred smiled blandly as Harry lifted Sarah down from her stool. 'Next time we see you it'll be Christmas, I expect. Unless you're off skiing again.'

Dan showed his teeth in a fleeting smile. 'I haven't planned that far ahead. See you later, Sarah.'

She included him in her general smile to everyone. 'Cheerio, gentlemen.'

Dan turned on his heel, and had gone through into the house before they'd reached the door.

'Was young Daniel bothering you?' said Harry, as they reached the pick-up.

'Not exactly. He just wanted to take me out to dinner again.'

'Again?'

'I had a meal with him on Monday night.'

'And you didn't want a repeat?'

Sarah smiled demurely. 'I'm seeing someone else tonight.'

He laughed. 'Good for you. Time you started going out a bit.'

'Exactly,' she agreed. 'But right now I'm off to contact the building surveyor.'

'I've been thinking, boss,' said Harry, as he drove away. 'Young Ian's not very happy with the firm he's working for now. What do you say to him coming in with us on the barns?'

Sarah's eyes lit up. 'I think it's a great idea, if he agrees. Find out what he's earning there and I'll see if I can pop it up a bit.'

'Right.' He got out to help her down when they reached Medlar House. 'I'll give you a ring later.'

'Thanks, Harry.'

His eyes twinkled. 'And you enjoy yourself tonight.'

Sarah spent some time on the phone for the rest of the afternoon. She contacted the offices of the building inspector, and arranged an appointment for the survey of the barns at Westhope Farm in two days' time. She rang Bob Grover with the news, and he assured her he'd be ready and waiting for the inspector, and promised to convey Sarah's good wishes to the new grandmother.

'What with your offer and the baby, Mavis is over the moon,' he said, chuckling. 'So am I, Miss Carver.'

Sarah typed a letter to confirm the inspection appointment at Westhope, then left a message on Oliver's phone to keep him up to date. Instead of driving she took a brisk walk to the Post Office stores to post her letter, and on the way back decided to forget about work for a while. Alex's visit had taken her by surprise last night, though to be fair she'd had plenty of time to tidy up before he arrived if she'd wanted. But tonight she would pull out all the stops. From the expression on Alex's face at the sight of her in a skirt, he obviously liked the girly look, so she'd keep to it tonight.

When she got back Sarah climbed the steps to her platform and slid back the doors on the wardrobe—which was so compact she'd sent a lot of her clothes to charity shops before moving in. She pushed aside the little black number and brought out the dress bought for her leaving party at the flat before moving from London.

Girly was the word for it, she thought with a grin later, as she zipped up the thin poppy-red voile. Slender straps held up the low-cut top, and the fluted skirt stopped just short of her knees. Sarah gave an excited little laugh as she looked at her reflection. Harry and his cronies wouldn't have recognised her. When the doorbell finally rang she went down the steps, carrying her shoes, feeling like Cinderella ready for the ball.

'I'm here,' said Alex.

Sarah buzzed him in, left her door ajar, then slid her feet into her shoes and stood in the middle of the room, waiting for him. He gave a perfunctory knock and came in, to stand very still just inside the door, looking pretty much perfect to Sarah in a linen jacket and khaki jeans which hugged his muscular thighs. They gazed at each other in silence, then, without taking his eyes away from her, Alex reached behind him to close the door.

'You look good enough to eat,' he said, in a tone which did damage to her pulse-rate.

'Thank you.'

'Would it endanger our embryo friendship if I kissed you?'

'You can if you're careful,' she said, offering her cheek.

'Sorry. Can't do careful,' he said, and kissed her mouth, taking so much time over it Sarah's heart was pounding by the time he raised his head. 'You know, I'm not so sure about this friend thing after all,' he said huskily, his eyes glittering.

She heaved in an unsteady breath, trying to damp down the heat his expert, hungry mouth had sent surging through her entire body. 'You don't want that any more?'

'Yes, of course I do. But I have a problem.'

'What?'

'The way you look tonight, any normal guy would want to be more than just your friend, Sarah. But don't worry,' he said softly. 'I'll stick to the rules.'

'What rules?'

'Yours: friendship with the enemy, but no sleeping with him.'

She eyed him quizzically. 'Is that what you want?'

He smiled wryly. 'Of course I do. I'd be lying if I said otherwise.'

'You're honest!'

'Always the best policy, Sarah. But don't let it worry you. Just good friends will do for now.' He touched a caressing finger to her bottom lip. 'So repair the damage, and let's take off to see what Stephen has to offer.'

Outside in the courtyard Sarah looked round for the Cherokee, her eyes wide as Alex led her to the classic beauty parked near the front gate.

'Wow,' she exclaimed. 'A Jensen Interceptor, no less. I do so hope my neighbours are watching. I got some teasing about the yellow Ferrari the other night, then Oliver collected me in his Daimler, and now you turn up with this baby.'

'My pride and joy, and used solely for special occasions,' said Alex, handing her in.

'I'm honoured. Though I would have been equally happy with the Jeep.'

'I know.' He slanted a smile at her. 'That's part of what makes the occasion special.'

It was Sarah's third meal in as many days at the Pheasant Inn, but eating alone with Alex raised the experience to a new level. His kiss earlier had altered things between them, to the point where just his mention of sleeping with the enemy was enough to revive sexual tension, which simmered below the surface while they studied menus and sipped the champagne he'd insisted on ordering.

'But the celebration was yesterday,' said Sarah, her colour rising as he looked into her eyes.

'This is to celebrate something far more important than mere business,' he said, toasting her. 'To friendship—among other things.'

'What other things?' she asked, raising her glass in response.

'Future pleasures.' He gave her the crooked smile that had once irritated her and now had a totally different effect. 'So, what would you like to eat?'

'I know it's a strange choice with champagne—I didn't dare

ask for it at lunch yesterday or Oliver would have had a stroke—but I fancy fish and chips.'

'You can have whatever you want,' Alex said, as the waitress arrived to take their order. 'I'll have the same.'

The simple, perfectly cooked food tasted wonderful, though Sarah had an idea that eating it in Alex's company had a lot to do with it. The small arrangement of flowers on the table had a single fat candle at its centre, with a flame which gave his eyes a more pronounced gleam than usual as they talked shop with the ease of old friends rather than recent enemies. Sarah's barn conversions were the main topic for a while, then she listened, fascinated, as Alex told her about the Merrick Group's acquisition of a manor house its owner no longer had the money to maintain.

'How sad,' said Sarah with compassion. 'To someone brought up to that kind of world it must be a bitter blow to leave it.'

'This particular owner grew up in a cottage much like the ones you've just developed. Ronnie Higgins, aka Rick Harmon, lead singer and guitarist of the Rampage, bought the house at the height of the group's success, but soon got too immersed in the good life to write new songs. The result was inevitable. Their records plummeted down the charts and the rainy day Rick never saved for arrived all too soon. He was forced to sell the fast cars, put the house up for sale and auction the contents.'

'Poor man. What will you do with it?'

'Convert it—with great sympathy—into luxury apartments. We've sold most of them in advance already.' Alex smiled. 'Would you like to live in something like that, Sarah?'

'No way.' She looked up with a smile as Stephen Hicks arrived to ask how they had enjoyed the meal.

'First class, as usual, Chef,' Alex assured him. 'The lady loves your fish and chips.'

Stephen rolled his eyes. 'Marvellous! I honed my craft in Paris and London, and all people want is my fish and chips.'

'I'll try whatever you recommend next time,' Sarah promised.

'You can tell us what to order when I book,' Alex assured his friend. 'What's for pudding?'

Sarah demurred, but gave in when Alex coaxed her to share a dish of sorbet made from blood oranges and pomegranates. She was actually dipping her spoon into their dish before the full intimacy of the process dawned on her. When his eyes held hers as he licked his spoon she felt a tide of red sweep up her face, and she swallowed another spoonful of icy perfection to tone it down.

'I think,' said Alex with constraint, 'that this was a mistake.'

'You want it all yourself?'

'No. But sharing it with you is giving me impure thoughts. Don't worry. I won't act on them.'

'Good.' Sarah laid her spoon down and sat back.

'You haven't eaten much!'

'I pigged on the fish and chips. I'd like some coffee instead, please.'

His eyes held hers. 'I was hoping for that when I take you home, Sarah.'

'Of course, but I'd like some right now just the same.' She smiled. 'And while we're waiting for it you can tell me more about Stephen. Is he an old schoolfriend?'

Alex shook his head. 'We met at Cambridge.'

'Did you read the same subjects?'

'No. His was Archaeology, mine Engineering. But we happened to meet on our first day, hit it off from the word go, and in our third year at Trinity we shared a double set—i.e. a communal living room with separate study/bedrooms.'

Sarah smiled, able to picture it only too well. 'I bet you had a fantastic time with all those clever girls around. Were there lots of parties?'

'Too many. Towards the end we had to buckle down to more serious stuff. Steve and I both played cricket, but like me he had parents who made sure he worked through vacations unless we were on tour.'

'Stephen couldn't have earned much on archaeological digs!'

'True. His Italian mother sent him off to Piedmont every summer, to work in her family's renowned cooking school.' Alex grinned. 'Steve's talent meant our dinner parties at Trinity were hot tickets.'

'So he never did anything with his archaeology?'

'No. As soon as he graduated he took off to France to cook.'

'And you went back home to the Merrick Group?'

'Exactly.' Alex smiled his thanks up at the waitress, and put a sizeable tip on the tray as she set the coffee pot in front of Sarah.

'Is it just coincidence that he opened a restaurant in this area?' she asked.

'No. After learning his craft in places like the River Café and the Savoy, he decided to open a place of his own. He asked me to keep a look out in this area, so when I heard through the grapevine that the Pheasant was going up for sale I told Steve to hotfoot it down here with Jane and take a look before it went on the open market.'

'You get on well with his wife?'

He nodded. 'Jane was at Trinity with us.'

A sort of private club, thought Sarah wistfully. 'Does she do any cooking?'

Alex laughed. 'None at all. That girl can burn water. She's the number-cruncher and takes care of the finances. She sees to the ordering, bullies the suppliers and does front of house. She's away at the moment, visiting her parents, but you can meet her next time.'

Stephen came out to intercept them as they were leaving. 'Nice to see you again, Sarah. Come again soon.'

'Not for a while,' said Alex with regret. 'I'm off to the London office tomorrow.'

'Which doesn't mean Sarah can't come here alone—or with someone else,' Stephen pointed out, and grinned at the look on his friend's face as he escorted them to the door.

On their way back, Alex shot a look at her. 'Would you do that?' he asked.

Sarah eyed him curiously. 'Would it matter to you if I did?'

'It would if it was Dan Mason.'

'How you do harp on about him. I won't go out with him again for the simple reason that I don't want to. But,' she warned, 'I refuse to boycott the Green Man just to avoid him. I enjoy my lunchtime sessions there.'

Alex touched a hand to hers. 'Dan must have gone back to the city by now.'

'He hasn't yet. He was still there when I went in with Harry today.'

'Was he, now? I wonder what's keeping him here so long this time,' said Alex as he turned into Medlar House.

'Could we stop talking about Dan Mason?' Sarah snapped, and stalked in front of him to open the main door. She unlocked her own door, switched on lamps and closed the shutters, then switched on her blinking answer-machine to hear Harry's familiar gruff tones telling her how much Ian earned. Sarah turned at last to find Alex watching her.

'I'll pass on more coffee.' He took her hand to lead her to the sofa, and slid a document from his pocket. 'I've sorted out storage for your furniture, so would you check the inventory Greg took this afternoon?'

'Oh—right. Thank you.' Sarah ran her eyes down the list, and nodded. 'That's the lot. Will you bill me?'

'No,' he said flatly. 'This is a personal arrangement between you and me, Sarah. So indulge me. Accept the storage rental as a gift from a friend.'

She smiled ruefully. 'I can hardly say no when you put it like that. Thank you, Alex.'

He leaned back, long legs outstretched. 'I could have stored it at my place, but I thought you might not go for that.'

'Harry pointed out the Merrick house to me on our way to Westhope. What I could see of it from the road was impressive. Is that where you live?'

'Not for years. When I was growing up we all lived there,

but my grandfather and Aunt Isabel are the only occupants these days. I've got a place of my own a few miles from here. I moved out of the family home when my mother left.'

'Do you see her often?'

'Yes, of course. She lives near Stratford-upon-Avon. I spend Christmas and New Year with her, and she comes to stay at my place quite a lot.'

Sarah turned her head to look at him curiously. 'Doesn't your father ever want you to spend Christmas with him?'

'Not since he's remarried. He takes his wife to a five-star hotel in a ski resort for New Year as her reward for enduring Christmas Day with my grandfather.'

'But you never stay home to endure it, too?'

'Old Edgar respects my wish to spend it with my mother. He doesn't care for her successor.'

'Do *you* like her?'

'We rub along.' Alex took her hand in his. 'Where do *you* spend Christmas?'

'It's not something I've looked forward to since my mother died. Oliver used to take Dad and me out to Christmas dinner at some hotel, rather than risk my cooking, and he still does the same now it's just the two of us.' Sarah smiled brightly. 'But let's change the subject. I'd much rather hear your views on quick-drying membranes for my barns.'

Alex threw back his head and laughed. 'Not a topic of conversation I've discussed with any other woman!'

'But one very dear to my heart right now. So, are you privy to any trade secrets I might find useful?'

For a while, only too happy to have Sarah hanging on to his every word, Alex obliged her with everything he knew on the subject—which was considerable. 'But now,' he said at last, 'let's talk about the weekend. I'll be back by then, so have lunch with me on Sunday. At my place, not the Pheasant.'

'Can you cook, then?'

'I was Stephen's *sous* chef often enough in the old days to learn a thing or two,' he assured her.

'In that case, thank you. I'd like to.'

'Good.' Alex took a card from his wallet. 'Here's my address. I've drawn a rough map on the back.'

Sarah eyed him narrowly as she took it. 'You were sure I'd come, then?'

'No. I lived in hope.' He got up with a sigh. 'I must go. Early start in the morning.'

'Are you staying with your father?'

He shook his head. 'When I'm in town I put up at the flat over the group offices.'

Sarah walked with him to the door. 'Thank you for this evening.'

'My pleasure—literally. Come about midday on Sunday—or I can drive over to fetch you?'

She shook her head. 'I'll enjoy the drive.' And could leave any time she wanted to.

Alex moved closer, smiling down at her. 'I've been very good. I deserve a goodnight kiss, Sarah.'

'In what way have you been good?' she asked lightly.

He took her in his arms. 'By not doing this again until now.' His lips met hers in a kiss which started off gently and then ignited into something so hot and intense Sarah was breathless by the time he released her. 'A goodnight kiss is allowable between friends,' he informed her, and kissed her again. 'Two, even,' he said not quite steadily. 'Goodnight, Sarah.'

'Goodnight.' She pressed the release for the outer door, and Alex smiled his crooked smile and went out into the hall, closing her door softly behind him.

CHAPTER EIGHT

NEXT DAY Sarah had nothing to do except think far too much about Alex Merrick's kisses. Until she heard from the building inspector there could be no progress at Westhope Farm. But in the meantime she would stop daydreaming and pass the time by dealing with laundry, spring-cleaning her flat, and even, horror of horrors, washing her mammoth windows.

She rang Harry after working on her laptop for a while, and told him she could top up Ian's present wage a little. 'Once I get the official report and make Mr Groves a firm offer, you can sound Ian out. If he's keen tell him to come round here to the flat one evening and we'll sort it.'

'He'll jump at it,' Harry assured her. 'So, what are you doing today, then?'

'Housework I haven't had time for lately,' said Sarah gloomily. 'Including the windows, heaven help me.'

'I'd better do that for you,' said Harry, to her astonishment. 'You'd be up and down a ladder like a monkey on a stick with the size windows you've got. Probably break a leg or something.'

'Harry, I can't ask you to clean my windows!'

'You didn't ask, I offered. I'll see you in half an hour,' he said firmly.

Only too happy to be relieved of the task she disliked most, Sarah loaded her washing machine and then got on with her cleaning, her mind on her evening with Alex. It was strange that dinner at the Pheasant with Dan Mason had merely been a way of killing time, whereas with Alex it had been pure pleasure from start to finish. Something she'd never felt with anyone before. Probably because he was nothing like the spoilt rich kid of her first impression. He'd worked hard to earn his crown. And he was no slouch in the kissing department either.

Sarah stood still in the middle of the room, her heart thumping again at the thought of Alex's kisses, until the doorbell brought her back to earth with a bump and she ran to open the door to Harry, who'd come armed with a telescopic ladder.

'Right then, boss, I'll get started.'

'This is very kind of you, Harry,' she said gratefully.

'I had nothing better to do. But not a word in the pub, mind,' he warned.

Sarah grinned. 'My lips are sealed. How about a cup of coffee before you start?'

'No thanks, I'll wait till I've finished. I'd better clean these shutters first,' he said, eyeing them. 'Might as well do the job properly. Got a bucket and some cloths?'

While Harry worked Sarah carried on with her own chores, and at intervals wrung out cloths for him and supplied fresh water. At last he stood back, eyeing pristine white shutters and gleaming glass with a grunt of satisfaction.

'All right if I go out through the long window?' he asked. 'Might as well do the outside and finish the job.'

'You're such a star, Harry,' Sarah said fervently.

'You'd best close the shutters a bit; I'll see better,' he said, and went out, pulling the window ajar behind him.

Sarah closed the shutters to halfway, then went up the steps to put fresh covers on her bed. She straightened in surprise at a knock on her door instead of the sound of the bell. She ran down, expecting one of her neighbours, and opened her door to find Dan Mason grinning down at her, so irritatingly sure of his welcome Sarah found it hard to summon a smile.

'Someone was delivering a parcel as I arrived so I sneaked in at the same time,' he said. 'Can I come in?'

Sarah nodded reluctantly, wishing she could say no.

Dan walked past her, looking impressed as he took in the proportions of the room. 'God, Sarah, what a place!'

'It was a music room originally, but I made some modifications.' Which was an understatement for a work programme which had started with tearing up lino and treating floorboards, progressed to building the windowseat and sleeping platform, and finished with the installation of her double row of shutters.

'But where do you sleep?'

'Up there,' Sarah said, waving a hand at the platform.

He raised an eyebrow. 'Romantic, but not much room for overnight guests.'

'None at all,' she said shortly. 'Why are you here, Dan?'

He smiled, moving closer. 'To get my request in early for your company at dinner tonight. Not the Pheasant again,' he added quickly. 'The weather's good, so we could drive to a place I know near Ross.'

She shook her head. 'That's very kind of you, Dan, but I've got something on tonight.'

'Two nights running with Alex Merrick?' he demanded, his bonhomie suddenly gone.

'As it happens, no.' Her chin lifted. 'But even if it were it's my business, Dan, no one else's.'

His mouth twisted. 'Oh, I get the message. The Crown Prince of Merrick strikes again. Alex always had the girls running after him. That smell of family money on him attracts them like flies. But he's a slippery customer; never gets hooked.' He caught her hands, sudden malevolence in his eyes. 'Did he score any better with you than I did?'

Sarah glared in disgust and tried to wrench free, but Dan jerked her into his arms and crushed his mouth down on hers. In furious, knee-jerk reaction she sank her teeth into his bottom lip, and he pushed her away with a howl of pain, a hand clapped to his mouth.

'Something wrong, Sarah?' said Harry, stepping through the window with his ladder. 'I thought I heard voices. Oh, it's you, Daniel.'

Dan was too taken aback at the sight of him to reply, his face like thunder as blood dripped down his chin.

Sarah fished a crumpled tissue from the pocket of her jeans. 'You'd better have this. You're bleeding.' She looked Harry in the eye. 'Dan tripped and caught his lip in his teeth.'

'Better get off home, then, Daniel,' advised Harry grimly. 'I'll see you to your car.'

'No need, Harry,' said Sarah. 'I'll do that.' She opened her door and waved Dan through, then marched across the hall to the main door. 'Is that why you came here, Dan? Because you heard I had dinner with Alex Merrick last night?'

He shrugged, his eyes like hard blue pebbles as he dabbed, wincing, at his lip. 'By the law of averages it might have been my turn to get lucky tonight.'

Sarah clenched her fists, itching to hit him. 'Not tonight, not ever, Dan Mason. Just go, please.'

'In my own good time,' he snarled.

'Right now, please, or I'll get Harry to speed you on your way.'

'What the hell's he doing here, anyway? Another of your conquests?'

'Oh, grow up, Dan,' she said wearily, and moved to close the main door, but he held up a hand.

'Be very careful where Alex Merrick's concerned, Sarah. At a stretch you could say you're both in the same line of business. But there's just one of you, while he's got his entire bloody group behind him.' He swore under his breath as Harry came out with his ladder.

'I'll just stow this in the pick-up before I have that coffee, boss.' Harry gave Dan a straight look. 'On your way now, are you, lad?'

Dan shot a venomous look at him as he stalked away to his

car, then with a growl of the powerful engine he drove off, barely stopping to check for traffic as he shot out into the road.

'Ed Mason spared the rod too much with that boy,' said Harry, walking back to Sarah. 'I was ready to haul him off you by the scruff of his neck, but you sorted him yourself. Good girl.'

'I try to be,' she said with a sigh. 'Let's have that coffee. I could even rise to a sandwich or two if you've got time to stay for a bit.'

After Harry left Sarah locked up her gleaming flat and went out. The incident with Dan had left a nasty taste in her mouth which would be best cured, she decided, by a trip into Hereford to buy herself something new to wear on Sunday. While she'd been working on the cottages an hour or two on a Saturday afternoon was the only time off she'd allowed herself, and she felt like a child let out of school as she drove into town on a week day.

After a tour of the chainstores in High Town, and diversions along narrow side streets to pricier shops, Sarah bought some delicacies from a food hall to add to her collection of carrier bags, found a couple of paperbacks after a browse in a bookshop, and finally drove out of the city just as rush hour was getting underway. When she got home she put the food away, and then climbed up the steps to put the rest of her shopping on the bed. It was at this point, she thought with a sigh, that she missed having a girlfriend on hand to give an opinion on the clothes she'd bought, or to try out the new lipstick.

Sarah shook off the mood. She had been the one desperate to work in a man's world, so she had no one to blame but herself. She had quite literally made her bed, so now she just had to lie on it. Alone, unfortunately. Unfortunately? She frowned as she hung up her new clothes. When she was building the platform had she deliberately given herself space for only a single bed, like a nun in a convent? Sarah snorted with laughter and went down to make supper.

Later, after Caesar salad and cherry tart bought earlier, Sarah took a stroll in the gardens before tackling a small mountain of ironing. At last, feeling pleasantly tired, she had just stretched out on the sofa to watch television when Alex rang.

'Hi,' she said, quite shaken by her delight at the sound of his voice. 'How's life in the big city?'

'Noisy. I miss the green and pleasant land of Herefordshire. What have you been doing today?'

'Cleaning, shopping—nothing much. How about you?'

'Meetings and more meetings.' Alex yawned. 'Sorry. Any progress on the barns?'

'The survey is booked for first thing in the morning, and the inspector promised to ring me with the result before sending me a written report.' She sighed. 'I'm an impatient soul. I couldn't bear the thought of a whole weekend without any news.'

Alex chuckled. 'So what will you do the moment you hear? Rush over to Westhope and press a cheque into Bob Grover's hand?'

'I shall conduct the sale in my usual businesslike manner.'

'Of which I have experience. You drove a hard bargain over the cottages.'

'Oh, come on, admit it. You got a really good deal there.'

'Fair, maybe, but I draw the line at really good! Now let's change the subject. Things have gone better today than expected, which means I'll be back on Saturday morning. Can you make it over to my place in time for dinner?'

'Instead of lunch on Sunday?'

'As well as, not instead of. Don't worry,' he added. 'I'll let you go home in between.'

'An offer I can't refuse.'

'I hope so.'

'Then I won't.'

'Won't come?'

'Won't refuse.'

'Seven sharp, then,' he said after a pause. 'Don't be late.'

* * *

Sarah went for a long walk next morning, while the inspection was taking place at Westhope Farm. But the phone in her pocket remained obstinately silent as she strolled through intersecting lanes she'd never had the time—or energy—to explore when she was working on the cottages. Eventually her route brought her back past the Post Office Stores. She bought a newspaper and bread and milk, chatted for a while with the owners, then started back at a leisurely pace. She was at home before her phone finally rang.

'Mark Prentiss here, Miss Carver.'

Her heart leapt. 'Hi, Mr Prentiss. Thank you so much for ringing. Don't keep me in suspense. What's the verdict?'

'Good. I did an inspection for Mr Grover in the first place,' he explained, 'so it was merely a case of checking my own work, with a few extras from your point of view. I'll get an official report sent off to you this afternoon.'

Sarah thanked him profusely, then rang Harry. 'We're on,' she said jubilantly. 'Once I get the written report I'll get my solicitor on board, then apply for the usual permits and it's all systems go. When can we pop over to see Mr Grover?'

'Now, if you like,' said Harry, and chuckled. 'Might as well give Bob and Mavis a happy weekend. I'll give them a ring, then come round to get you.'

After her long walk in the morning, topped by her euphoria over the inspection, and then Mavis Grover's vast high tea washed down with parsnip wine, Sarah fell asleep on the drive back, and came to with a start when Harry turned into the courtyard of Medlar House.

'Sorry, Harry,' she said with contrition.

'Too much excitement,' he said, helping her down. 'Watch your step. Mavis's wine is powerful stuff.'

'Tell me about it!' Sarah swayed on her feet as the cool

evening air hit her. 'Wow. I couldn't refuse it because you were driving, but I hope I don't have a hangover tomorrow.'

'Drink a lot of water and a few cups of tea and you'll be fine,' he told her. 'Best get to bed early.'

Sarah nodded, then clutched her head, wishing she hadn't. 'Thank you, Harry. Talking of tea, can I make you some before you go?'

'No, thanks. I'm off down the pub for a game of cribbage with Fred.'

'You can mention the barns to him on the quiet, if you like. And bring Ian round for a chat about the job as soon as Mr Selby has everything legally sorted. I think your sister was very pleased,' she added, smiling.

'Pleased?' Harry gave a snort of laughter. 'I wouldn't mind betting she's taking a glass or two more of her parsnip wine right now. Bob, sensible chap, sticks to beer.'

'You think they were satisfied with my offer?'

'More than satisfied,' he assured her, and jingled his car keys. 'It was a really nice thought to buy that teddy bear for the baby, boss.'

'I had fun choosing it, Harry. Enjoy your game.'

Her house phone was ringing when Sarah let herself into the flat.

'Hi,' said Alex.

'Oh, it's you,' she said in relief.

'Yes, me. Disappointed?'

'Quite the reverse.' She'd been afraid it was Dan Mason 'But normally you ring me on my mobile.'

'I tried. No luck.'

'I left my phone behind when I went to Westhope. Wish me luck, Alex. I just climbed on the second rung of the property ladder.'

'Congratulations! We'll celebrate tomorrow night.' He sighed. 'I would have come back tonight and called in on you but I'm dining—reluctantly—in the bosom of my family. My father was so insistent I gave in for once.'

'Think of the filial glow you'll bask in!'

'I'd rather think of tomorrow evening with my new best friend.'

'I thought Stephen Hicks was your best friend.'

'He is. But you have a big advantage over him.'

'What's that?'

'You're a girl.'

'Tut-tut, you can't say that these days, Mr Merrick. I'm a woman,' Sarah chastised.

'That too. Though it's hard to believe when you're wearing those overalls.'

'How you do harp on about them. Anyway, I bought some new ones yesterday. I went shopping in Hereford.'

'Not just for work clothes, surely. What else did you buy?'

'A teddy bear with a blue bow tie.'

'Original—dinner guests normally bring wine!'

'It's for the Grovers' brand-new grandson,' she said, laughing.

'Pity. I quite fancy the teddy—hell, I just noticed the time. Got to go, Sarah. Be punctual tomorrow.'

'I will be, if your directions are accurate.'

'Of course they are. You can't miss it. Turn left past the church, follow the signs for Glebe Farm, and my place is the first turning on the right.'

'I'll ring if I get lost.'

'Why not just let me come and fetch you?'

'I'd rather come under my own steam.'

'So you've got a getaway car if you need to escape?'

'Of course not,' she lied. 'See you tomorrow.'

CHAPTER NINE

By the time she was ready the following evening Sarah was running late. Far too much time had been wasted in trying to tame her hair, also dithering about whether to wear the new stretch sequin mini-dress on its own. In the end she lost her nerve, wore it over slim white jeans and locked up the flat. She tossed a long cardigan and a rain jacket in the back of her car, propped Alex's directions on the dashboard and set off.

The journey was more complicated than it looked on his diagram, but eventually she came to the church he'd marked and turned down a lane with a sign for Glebe Farm. She took the first turning on the right, as instructed, her eyes like saucers when she spotted Alex leaning against a gate in front of a large and very beautiful barn conversion. The sleeves of his blue chambray shirt were rolled up, his faded old jeans fitted him very exactly, and his eyes danced as he waved her through. He shut the gate and sprinted after her as she drove on to park in the forecourt between two mushroom-shaped stones in front of the building.

Alex opened her door and gave her a quick kiss as he helped her out. 'You're late, but welcome anyway.'

'You never thought to mention you lived in a barn conversion?' she demanded hotly.

'Of course I did, but I decided to spring it on you as a surprise instead.'

'Is this the only one on the farm?'

'The only conversion, anyway. Matt Hargreaves uses the other barns for their original purpose, and sold me this one years ago. His farm is half a mile down the road, so I buy milk and eggs from him, but otherwise I don't get in his way much.'

Sarah leaned against the car, taking in every detail of his home's beautifully maintained exterior. Glass panels had replaced the wood in the original barn doors, and a flight of worn stone steps led up alongside the entrance porch to a window set in the former entrance to the old hayloft.

'It's just wonderful, Alex,' she said with a sigh, and smiled at him. 'Come on, then. Give me the guided tour.'

He opened the porch door into a small entrance hall with a small shower room to one side of it, and mouth-watering dinner smells coming from a kitchen on the other. 'The rest is through here.' He ushered her into a vast, open-plan space with a vaulted ceiling and exposed beams. Light poured through the tall glass doors and from the windows at the rear, highlighting the treads of a spiral stair which wound up in shallow, leisurely curves to a galleried landing. To one side of the staircase on the ground floor a handsome stone fireplace had been built into the end wall. In front of it a Persian rug in glowing colours warmed the stone floor between a pair of sofas with end-tables and lamps, and a carved cupboard against the outer wall. In the other half of the room the wall backed a long credenza table, and solid oak chairs were grouped round a long refectory table already laid for dinner, with an open bottle of wine and a board with a rustic looking loaf and a hunk of cheese already in place.

The first, overwhelming impression was of space and light. Sarah gazed up in rapture at the vaulted ceiling. 'I'm so impressed by the way you've done the beams, Alex.'

'They were too dark as they were, so I had them stripped and treated, then lime-washed to get this bleached effect. The idea was to look almost like a ghost of the original structure. Would you like to see the bedrooms?' added Alex, watching her face.

Sarah nodded eagerly, and started up the stairs. Along with his enjoyment of her trim back view, Alex felt a deep sense of satisfaction as he followed her. Unless he was much mistaken, Sarah Carver lusted after his house. Just as he'd hoped. The next step was to get her to lust after its owner. No, he thought, frowning. Not lust. That was too raw and basic for the feelings he wanted to arouse in her. Not that thinking of arousal of any kind was a good idea right now, when he was about to show her his bedroom.

Sarah stood at the gallery rail, admiration in her eyes as she gazed down at the floor below. 'Did you do all this yourself?'

'I was involved at every stage, certainly,' he said, leaning beside her. 'The interior design is mine, the staircase and so on. And the extra windows. Like you, I'm hooked on light and space.'

Sarah shook her head. 'My room can hardly compare with this.'

'But you worked on it yourself, so it's your baby as much as this place is mine. I used to slog away here every weekend I could, and the occasional evening when the job allowed. Some weekends Kate Hargreaves took pity on me, and sent a hot meal over from the farm.' Alex shrugged. 'My father left to oversee the manufacturing side from the London office soon after I acquired this place, so I didn't have too much time to spare for building work.'

'Did you have a pleasant evening, by the way?'

'Relatively, yes.' Alex took her hand. 'Take a look at the bedrooms, then I'll feed you.'

To offset the dark wood of his plain, masculine bedroom furniture, the bedcovers in all the rooms were white. The master bedroom was large, as Sarah had expected, but the two guest rooms were anything but small, and all three had their own bathrooms, fitted to a standard her practised eye could now price very accurately.

'My father thinks I went overboard with the white look,' said Alex. 'Too stark and monastic for his taste. His place in London leans to opulence and colour.'

'I think yours is exactly right,' said Sarah, and smiled at him. 'Will you object if I take a leaf out of your book and do something similar at Westhope?'

'I'll consider myself flattered.' He went out on to the landing, beckoning her to follow. 'Come on, let's eat. I'll just throw some pasta in a pot and dinner will be ready.'

Sarah smiled as she followed him down the elegant curving stair. In the past the only meal a man had ever made for her had been pasta with sauce from a jar. Apparently the vice-chairman of the Merrick Group was no more inventive in his smart kitchen than the boyfriends who had worried her father so much at one time.

Alex pulled out a chair at the dining table. 'Sit down, madam, and I shall bring in the food in exactly five minutes.'

'What are we having?'

'Nothing fancy.' Alex lit two candles in heavy glass holders and went off to the kitchen. When he came back with two steaming bowls, Sarah received hers with a mental apology to the chef.

'*Gnocchi di patate pomodoro e rucola*,' he announced grandly. 'Potato dumplings with tomato sauce and rocket.' He poured the wine and sat down, smiling at her as he raised his glass. 'Your health, Sarah.'

'Yours too,' she said, toasting him. She eyed her meal with respect. 'This looks—and smells—wonderful.' She drank some wine, grated cheese over the *gnocchi*, and then put the first fluffy, melting forkful in her mouth. 'Mmm,' she said indistinctly, as the flavour of the sauce hit her tastebuds. 'It tastes wonderful, too.'

'Good. I enjoy seeing a woman eat.'

'It's one of my favourite pastimes!'

Alex eyed her curiously. 'What are the others?'

She looked up from her plate. 'Other what?'

'Pastimes.'

Sarah thought about it. 'I enjoy my work so much I suppose you could list that as a pastime. I don't seem to have time for anything else other than reading—at least not in summer. This winter I'm going to make an effort to go to concerts and plays, and visit exhibitions and so on. Last winter I was too busy fitting up my flat to go out much, except for a couple of weekends I spent in London with former flatmates.'

'You've been back only twice?'

'The first weekend was fine, because I hadn't been gone long. But the second weekend was a mistake because by that time I was totally out of the loop.' Sarah shrugged. 'Once you're gone, you're gone.'

'These weren't close friends, obviously?'

'No, but I'll always be grateful to them, because they were kind to me after Dad died. I shared their flat after the family home was sold.' She looked at him expectantly as she went on eating. 'What kind of things do *you* do in your spare time?'

Alex smiled ruefully. 'I used to play village cricket, but these days I can't count on being free for net practice sessions, or even for a match itself, so I've given it up and run a bit instead. I cycle as well, but sometimes life's so hectic that lately I've been glad just to potter in my bit of garden on a Sunday, or watch cricket instead of actually playing.'

'You must have more of a social life than that!'

'Corporate entertaining mostly.' His mouth turned down. 'I get invited to private dinner parties quite a bit, too, but I accept only if I'm sure there's no catch.'

Sarah looked at him for a moment. 'A helping hand for the host's career?'

He shook his head. 'Unwilling partner for the hostess's single best friend.'

'Tricky! That kind of dinner party doesn't feature in my life,' said Sarah thankfully. She eyed the rustic loaf. 'I'd love a chunk of that to wipe out my bowl.'

Alex laughed, and jumped up to cut it for her. 'We'll both have some.'

Sarah mopped up every last drop of sauce with her bread,

then sat back, licking her lips. 'It's a sin to waste any of that sauce.' She smiled sweetly. 'How clever of you to make *gnocchi*. I've heard it's a pretty ticklish process. You must give me your recipe.'

Alex got up to refill her glass, but Sarah shook her head.

'No more; I've got to drive home.'

'Confession time.' His eyes gleamed in the candlelight that burned brighter now it was darkening rapidly outside. 'I made the sauce from scratch, I swear, but Steve gave me the *gnocchi*. I called in on my way home this morning and asked if he had any fresh pasta to spare, but he said his *gnocchi* would impress you more than the usual spaghetti.'

Sarah laughed. 'He was right. It was delicious.'

'Stay where you are,' he added as he collected plates. 'Dinner's not over yet.'

Sarah looked round with envy when he'd disappeared into the kitchen, liking the idea of a next time. She felt so at home here. Probably because on a grander scale the vaulted ceiling and open space gave the same sense of breathing room as her flat.

Alex came in to switch on lamps. 'It's raining hard out there.'

Sarah could hear it drumming on the roof as he went to fetch the next course. It gave her the feeling of security experienced in childhood when she'd been tucked up in bed listening to rain spattering against the windows. She smiled at Alex as he came back. 'I love that sound.'

'So do I.' He put a tray on the table, with coffee and a luscious looking dessert. 'I cadged this from Steve, too. Chocolate and almond tart. You'll like it.'

Sarah did like it. So much that she gave in to temptation and accepted another slice. 'But just a sliver, or I won't get into these jeans again.'

'Which would be a pity,' he said blandly, 'when they're such a perfect fit.'

She grinned. 'I suppose you noticed when you were following me up the stairs?'

'A man can't help noticing such things,' said Alex, unrepentant. 'Will you pour?'

They lingered over coffee until the pot was dry, while Sarah listened avidly to Alex's account of his work on the house. But at last he apologised for getting carried away and stacked their cups on the tray. 'Now, you take a sofa over there while I clear away.'

'I'll help,' she said firmly, and started gathering up dessert plates.

While they tidied up, in his compact, well-designed kitchen, Alex demanded a detailed account of her movements since he'd last seen her, and Sarah told him about the meal at Westhope Farm, and Mavis Grover's powerful parsnip wine. But they were sitting on one of the sofas together before she mentioned Dan Mason's visit.

'He came round to your place?' Alex's eyes narrowed. 'And what was that about?'

'He wanted me to have dinner with him again, at some place near Ross.'

'And what did you say?' he asked silkily.

'I said no. And not just because you warned me against him, so don't look so smug.' Sarah shivered. 'I didn't want to go out with him, to Ross or anywhere else.'

'Good,' said Alex with satisfaction, and put an arm round her.

'Dan was so objectionable when I said no—Harry was all for seeing him off,' she added, chuckling. 'He'd been cleaning my windows. You should have seen Dan's face when Harry appeared.'

'Good for Harry!'

'Anyway, Dan went off in a huff, but his parting shot was a warning about you.'

Alex stiffened. 'Oh?'

'He said I should watch my step, because I'm in the same line of business as you, and while I'm just small fry you've got the might of the Merrick Group behind you.'

'That's nonsense,' he said flatly. 'The man's an idiot.'

'He also told me,' Sarah informed him, 'that droves of

women are attracted to your Merrick money, but you refuse to get hooked.'

Alex's mouth curled in distaste. 'I think *droves* may be exaggerating slightly. Besides, I did get hooked. Once.'

'Do you still have feelings for the lady? Sorry,' she added hastily. 'You don't have to answer that.'

'My pride took a beating at the time. But it recovered, and so did I. Completely.' He smiled crookedly 'Unlike those mythical droves of women, mere money doesn't work for you, Sarah, does it? Least of all when it comes attached to the name of Merrick.' He leaned nearer. 'But you wouldn't be here tonight if you didn't like me for myself a little.'

'True. I do like you. And not just a little. I like you a lot.' On impulse she kissed his cheek.

Alex promptly seized her in his arms and kissed her mouth, and when she made no protest went on kissing her with a savouring pleasure she shared to the full. 'I can stop if you like,' he whispered, after an interval.

Sarah shook her head. 'Not just yet. Kiss me some more.'

'Yes, ma'am!' He ran the tip of his tongue round her parted lips, then slid it between them in a caress which she responded to with such fervour he lifted her onto his lap as he kissed her. He felt a surge of triumph as her breath quickened in time with his. He smoothed a hand over the glittering fabric covering her breasts, and felt himself harden as her breath caught. He raised his head, his eyes questioning. 'You don't like that?'

She nodded wordlessly, her breathing ragged as his mouth returned to hers, coaxing and tasting with a new hunger as his caressing fingers slid beneath the tunic to trace the shape of breasts which were suddenly so taut and sensitive she felt fire streak south to parts of her unused to such ravishing sensation. Then suddenly she was back in her place on the sofa, and Alex was on his feet, raking a hand through his hair.

'Look, Sarah, let's get something straight. Just because I

asked you to come to my place doesn't mean I expect you to sing for your supper.'

'That's a relief,' she said breathlessly, 'because I can't carry a tune in a bucket.'

He let out a crack of laughter and sat down again. 'No singing, then. I'm not trying to rush you to bed, either.'

Sarah took in a deep, calming breath. 'If you had something like that in mind you'd do better to stick to a sofa down here. It must be a bit tricky to rush someone up that stairway of yours.'

Alex moved closer and took her hand. 'I've never tried, but you're probably right.'

She gave him a thoughtful look. 'Funny, really. Neither of us owns easily accessible bedrooms. And in my case, even when you get up to the platform, the bed is too narrow to take more than one person.'

'And one small person at that,' he said, smoothing a finger over the back of her hand. 'For my part, I suppose I took it for granted that if ever I did invite a lady to sleep here she'd climb the stair willingly. And of course the lady who does sleep here on a regular basis does exactly that. My mother,' he added.

Sarah smiled, hoping he hadn't noticed her fleeting pang before the penny dropped. 'She must be very proud of what you've done here.'

He nodded, his eyes softening. 'She saw it at various stages on her visits—which, by the way, are not solely to catch up with me. She spends time with my aunt and grandfather as well. The old reprobate positively dotes on her. Which explains his attitude to my charming stepmother.'

'It's an awkward situation,' agreed Sarah. 'Have they ever met? Your mother and stepmother, I mean?'

'Oh, yes, they've met—' Alex's grip tightened as lightning lit up the room, followed by an earth-shattering crack of thunder. He smiled at her. 'That was close.'

She nodded, heart thumping.

'Are you afraid of storms?'

'Not afraid, exactly,' she lied, 'as long as I'm under cover. I don't like being out in them.' She winced as another flash lit the room, followed by another crack of thunder.

'You certainly won't be going out in this one. I have two spare bedrooms, Sarah.'

She gasped as lightning and thunder did their double act again, and Alex put his arms round her. 'Thank you,' she said against his chest. 'I'll take you up on that. I don't fancy driving home in this.'

He held her closer as the storm grew in intensity, and chuckled as the next clap of thunder sent her burrowing against him. 'From a purely personal point of view, I'm grateful to the weather.'

Sudden torrential rain blotted out conversation, and Alex raised Sarah's face to his and kissed her. She wreathed her arms round his neck and kissed him back with a fervour he returned with such intensity that Sarah forgot about the storm. Then lightning lit up the room, followed by a crash louder than anything that had gone before, and the lights went out.

Sarah let out a deep, unsteady breath as Alex released her.

'At least we've got the candles on the table to see by, but sit still and don't move,' he told her. 'I'll see if it's just the trip-switch, in which case I can trip it back on. If not we'll need torches and more candles.' He gave her a swift kiss and got up.

'Don't be long,' said Sarah involuntarily.

'I'll be back in a flash,' he promised, then laughed as lightning lit the room again. 'Right on cue, but the thunder's not so close this time.'

Sarah counted to five before the expected crack reverberated through the room, and she relaxed slightly, chuckling when Alex cursed as he stumbled over something in the kitchen. He came back with a box holding candles and torches.

'Not just the trip-switch, I'm afraid. There must be a line down somewhere—not unusual in these parts.' He set a torch down on the table beside Sarah, put the box on the floor and fetched the candles from the dining table. He put them down at either end of the sofa, then took matches and a selection of saucers out of the box. 'I own just the two candle holders, so otherwise I make do with these.'

'Does this happen regularly, then?'

'Enough to make it sensible to have this kind of thing on hand.' He glanced at his watch. 'It's a bit late to ring my aunt to see if Edgar's all right. But I've told her I'm home, so she'll ring me if he's not.' Alex handed her a candle and saucer and struck a match, and Sarah held the wick in the flame and waited until wax dripped enough for her to secure the candle in the saucer.

When they had four candles alight Alex ranged them along the fireplace, then sat down again. 'Now, where were we?' he said, and pulled her onto his lap, smiling into her eyes. 'I think I was doing this,' he whispered, and kissed her as though the simple, ravishing pleasure of the kiss itself was all he needed or intended.

It was Sarah, to her surprise, who grew impatient first. She wriggled closer on his lap, and Alex groaned and held her still.

'I'm only human,' he whispered against her lips.

'So am I,' she whispered back.

As though her words had triggered some switch inside him, his mouth suddenly devoured hers, their hearts thumping so madly in unison as he crushed her close that Sarah longed to tell Alex to forget any scruples and take her to bed. A shiver ran through her as his hands slid up under the stretchy sequinned fabric, and she stopped thinking altogether as his fingertips played such clever, inciting games with her sensitised nipples that she dug her fingers into his back in demand.

Alex raised his head, his eyes dark 'This,' he said hoarsely, 'is the part where I wish I had an ordinary flight of stairs so I could do the Rhett Butler thing and carry you up to bed to ravish you.' He set her on her feet and stood up, rejoicing as he saw the glittering sequins moving in hurried rhythm with her breathing. 'Instead,' he said, holding her eyes, 'I'm going to take you by the hand and lead you up those stairs to my room—and then ravish you.'

'In that case,' said Sarah breathlessly, 'you'd better blow out these candles.'

Alex pulled her close. 'You approve my plan?'

She nodded. 'If you'd said you just wanted to make love to me I might have said no, but ravishing sounds too good to pass up.'

Laughing together, they blew out the candles in the saucers, then took the pair in the glass holders up the winding stair to the master bedroom.

Alex kissed her swiftly. 'Wait there. I'll go down and get the torches.' When he came back with them he put a bottle of wine down alongside the candles, took a glass from each of his pockets and placed them by the wine. 'Since you're not driving anywhere tonight, I thought you might like another glass of this.'

She beamed at him. 'I would. Thank you.'

Alex sat on the edge of the bed and patted the place beside him. 'Come and sit here and I'll pour.'

Sarah kicked off her sandals and perched beside him. He gave her a glass of wine, then took her free hand in his and kissed it fleetingly.

'This is a very good idea,' she told him, as thunder rumbled in the distance.

'I get them sometimes,' he said modestly, and stroked a hand down the sequins. 'I like this sexy chainmail thing you're wearing.'

'It's a dress,' she informed him.

'So why are you wearing jeans with it?'

'It's shorter than my usual stuff.'

Alex grinned, his eyes gleaming wickedly in the candle-light. 'If the dress is short on you, it must be a bit dangerous on taller women.'

Sarah nodded. 'It's meant to be. The woman in the shop said it looked perfect, but then, that's her job.' She sipped more of her wine. 'This is delicious—and hopefully a lot less lethal than Mavis Grover's parsnip wine. When Harry drove me home from Westhope I fell asleep in the pick-up.'

'If at all possible,' said Alex, his hand tightening on hers,

'I'd rather my wine doesn't have the same effect on you. At least not yet.'

Sarah chuckled. 'Before you ravish me, you mean?'

'Exactly!' He slid an arm round her, and pulled her close with a sigh of pleasure. 'This is a very good way to spend Saturday night.'

'Except for the storm.'

'Because of the storm,' he contradicted. 'Otherwise we wouldn't be here on my bed together, and you would probably be driving home by now.'

'True.' Sarah raised her glass in solemn toast. 'To the storm.' She drank the rest of her wine and handed him the glass.

Alex laid it on the side-table with his, then piled his pillows at the head of the bed and pulled her up into his arms as he leaned against them, his breath warm and tingling against her ear. 'To make it even more perfect, would you do something for me?'

Sarah angled her face up to his. 'Sing, or recite from Shakespeare maybe?'

'Later for that. Right now I want to see you in the dress without the jeans.'

She slid off the bed and stood up. Aware in every fibre of his gleaming, intent eyes, she unzipped the jeans and took them off. Deliberately taking her time about it, she folded them and placed them on the chest between the windows, then gave a smothered gasp as he pounced on her and carried her back the bed.

'Is this where I get ravished?' she demanded. 'Because if it is I'll take the dress off too. It was expensive.'

'I'll do it for you.' He took the glittering garment very carefully by the hem and drew it over her head, then laid it over the back of a chair.

Sarah tried to relax against the pillows, but it was difficult when she was breathless, shaking inside, and hot all over even though all she was wearing were some lacy bits of nude satin that had cost more than the dress.

Alex stood very still and tense at the foot of the bed, his eyes so openly eating her up that Sarah held up her arms and he dived across the bed to scoop her up against him. He kissed her hungrily and Sarah kissed him back with equal fervour, one part of her admiring his skill as he removed his clothes without taking his lips from hers, the other part of her hot with anticipation as he drew back to gaze down at her. The possessive look in his eyes was as tactile as the caress of his stroking hands. Then his mouth moved down her throat and she lay with closed eyes, quivering as his lips moved in a slow, erotic trail down her throat, and over her shoulders, her anticipation mounting as he neared the swell of her breasts. Suddenly she pushed him away, her eyes glittering in her flushed face.

'What's wrong?' he whispered.

'Nothing at all. It's my turn. I want to look at you.' Sarah smiled, open relish in her eyes as they moved inch by inch over his broad chest and flat-planed stomach.

She leaned nearer to trail caressing hands down the same path, well aware of the effect they were having on him, and when she laid her open mouth against his chest he pulled her hard against him, his patience gone. With unsteady hands he removed the scraps of satin, and at last they were naked in each other's arms, their kisses frantic as their bodies came into contact. The breath tore through her chest as his lips left hers, his hair brushing her hot skin as he used his mouth on her breasts. She shivered at the touch of his tongue and grazing teeth, then gave a stifled moan as he parted her thighs to cause such unbearable arousal with his caresses her entire body felt bathed in flames.

He leaned away for a moment, then let himself down on her very gently, until every part of his body was touching every part of hers. She gazed up at him, her eyes lambent with invitation, then gasped in delight against his possessive mouth as he slid slowly home inside her. She made a relishing sound deep in her throat, her body taking its lead from his as he made love to her with all the care and skill at his command, until her urgent hips stole the last of his control and he took her at thrusting, break-neck speed towards the goal he reached at last before her. Still erect and throbbing with his own release, he drove deeper and held her impaled until he felt her climax ripple around him, then he collapsed on her, his face buried in her hair.

When Sarah found the energy to move at last she yelped in pain, because her hair was trapped. Alex kissed her in apology as he freed her and brushed the tangled curls back from her face, then slid off the bed to make for the bathroom.

'Well?' he said softly, when he rejoined her. 'Did you enjoy being ravished?'

'I don't think you could describe it that way,' she said, thinking it over.

Alex looked down at her, frowning. 'You mean I fell short of expectations?'

She rolled her eyes. 'Typical man!' She touched a hand to his cheek. 'Of course you didn't. But ravishing implies that the woman is unwilling in some degree. And, as perhaps you noticed, I wasn't. Unwilling, I mean.'

'I noticed,' he said, with deep satisfaction.

Sarah looked at him steadily. 'I didn't know it could be like that, Alex.'

The intense, dark-rimmed gaze held hers. 'How much experience have you had?'

'Not nearly as much as you, I imagine,' she said tartly. A very few episodes in the past, where enthusiasm had featured far more than skill, hardly counted. Whereas at Cambridge alone a man like Alex must have been able to take his pick of the women students. And probably of the damsels at Medlar House before he'd even left school.

'I'm no Casanova,' he assured her, reading her mind, then laughed suddenly into her neck.

'What's so funny?'

'I've just noticed that the storm has gone and the lights are on downstairs, and I think they've been on for some time.'

CHAPTER TEN

SARAH LAUGHED, but stayed his hand as he reached to turn on the bedside lamp. 'Not just yet. Leave me with romantic candlelight for a while.'

Alex slid from the bed to fetch a dressing gown from his wardrobe. 'What would you like? More wine? Or now we have power again I could make coffee.'

'Could you make tea instead?' Sarah said hopefully, controlling an urge to dive under the quilt now Alex was covered and she was not.

'I certainly could. Anything else?'

'My handbag. It's near the sofa somewhere.'

'Right. I won't be long.' Alex bent to plant a swift kiss on her mouth. 'Don't go away.'

Sarah made a beeline for the bathroom, for the swiftest shower on record, then wrapped herself in the towelling robe hanging behind the door. She switched on the bedside lamps and blew out the candles, tidied the bed, and went barefoot downstairs just as Alex came into the main room from the kitchen, carrying a loaded tray.

'What the blazes are you doing down here?' he demanded. 'I was just coming up to you with the tea.'

'I couldn't let you carry it up that staircase when I can drink it just as well down here on the sofa.' She smiled, relieved when his eyes softened.

'I usually take a tray up to bed on a Sunday morning,' he informed her, and raised that eyebrow again. 'At least you're still here. While I was making tea and so on, I wondered if I'd find you dressed and ready to leave when I took it up to you.'

Sarah flushed. 'I can still do that, if you like.'

Alex stalked to the table beside the sofa and put the tray down so hard the cups rattled. 'No. I do not like. I wanted you to stay in my bed so I could rejoin you there. Not necessarily for more sex—though I wouldn't say no—but just to stay there together until we went to sleep.' He cast a look at the robe. 'A trifle large, but it looks good on you.'

'I hope you don't mind,' she said awkwardly. 'I had a very quick shower.'

'I certainly do mind. If I'd known I would have postponed the tea-making and had one with you.'

'I seem to be getting things wrong here,' she said crossly. 'You'll have to forgive me, Mr—'

He held up a hand. 'Don't!'

'I was going to say,' she went on with dignity, 'that I'm not sure of the right procedure on these occasions. My former brushes with—with romance were not sleepovers.'

Alex's eyebrows rose. 'Are you saying you've never slept with a man?'

'Yes,' she said shortly, and picked up her bag.

'You've changed your mind about leaving?' he said sharply.

'No. I just want to slap some moisturiser on my face.' She glared at him. 'If that's all right with you.'

He took in a deep breath. 'Let's start again. Sarah—my darling Sarah—come back to bed with me to drink your tea.'

She thought it over. 'OK.' She glanced at the teapot. 'But I'd better carry that.'

'Off you go, then. I promise not to leer at your back view while I follow.'

'Not much to leer at in this dressing gown!'

Alex smiled. 'Ah, but I know exactly what's under it.' To his delight Sarah flushed hectically, snatched the teapot from the tray and marched over to the stairs.

When Sarah had said yes to dinner at home with Alex, she'd known perfectly well that dinner was probably not the only thing he had in mind. And if bed was involved she had been prepared for that. Welcomed it, looked forward to it, had been so excited by the prospect she'd put new underwear at the top of her shopping list for her trip to Hereford. But her imagination had never gone as far as picturing the fun of a midnight feast in bed with him. It was long past midnight by this time, but the principle was the same. She curled up against his banked pillows, smiling when he offered her thick slices of buttered toast.

'No wonder I had time to shower if you were getting this together,' she commented as he handed her a plate.

'I'm hungry,' he said simply, and smiled. 'Are you still cross with me, or will you eat some of this?'

'I'm not cross.' She grinned at him as she took a couple of slices. 'In fact I'm flattered. *And* I'm hungry. Even though after dinner I was sure I wouldn't eat again for at least a day.' She drank the tea he gave her in one draught.

'You were thirsty,' said Alex, and got up to take her cup as she began to eat.

'I'm amazed you have a teapot,' she commented, watching him pour.

He grinned. 'It was a present from my aunt when I moved in, with instructions to serve tea properly to my mother. In cups, with saucers.'

Sarah relaxed against the pillows as they ate. 'I didn't expect all this when I said yes to dinner,' she told him.

'Expect what, exactly?' He took her cup and plate away and stacked them with his own on the tray, then brushed crumbs from the covers and sat back beside her. 'Making love with me?'

Sarah turned to look at him. 'That did occur to me.'

His eyes held hers. 'Yet you still came?'

'Yes.'

'Is it remotely possible that you wanted it to happen?'

She gave him a smile as crooked as his. 'I thought you might have picked up certain clues about that.'

Alex slid his arm round her and drew her close. 'Let's see. First you actually turned up. Second you fell madly in love with my house. True?'

'Oh, yes,' she sighed, rubbing her cheek against his shoulder.

Alex's arm tightened. 'Then you kissed me of your own accord. On the cheek, admittedly, but a voluntary kiss for all that. I was, to put it mildly, encouraged.' He dropped a kiss on her hair. 'The storm finally clinched it. And here we are, *on* if not *in* my bed, relaxing in the aftermath of what I can only describe—poetic fool that I am—as a trip to heaven and back. How am I doing? Is there anything I missed?'

'The underwear.'

His eyebrow rose. 'I noticed it was pretty mouth-watering before I parted you from it, but is there more to it than that?'

She nodded. 'Normally I wear a chainstore white cotton bra, and the kind of knickers that come three in a pack. I bought the sexy stuff specifically to wear today.'

Alex put a finger under her chin to turn her face up to his. 'To seduce me?' he said incredulously.

'Of course not,' she said impatiently. 'But I thought there was a possibility you might want to seduce *me*.' Her eyes fell. 'And if you did,' she muttered, 'I wanted to look good.'

'*Good?* I wanted to fall on you and gobble you up,' he growled, and kissed her hard. 'I still do,' he said, and threw off his dressing gown and laid a hand on the tie securing hers. 'Do you want me to?'

'Yes,' she tersely, and abandoned any last lingering inhibitions to show him how much.

When Sarah surfaced again it was daylight. She found an arm round her waist, and a long, muscular leg hooked over both of hers, and opened her eyes on Alex's intent gaze.

'Good morning,' he said softly.

'Good morning.' She blinked sleepily. 'What time is it?'

'Just after nine. Want some breakfast?'

She thought it over. 'Could I have another shower first?'

'Certainly.' Alex slid to his feet and scooped her up in his arms. 'But this time I'm sharing.'

The shower involved a great deal more than just getting clean, and led them straight back to bed, and to lovemaking that was different from the night before. Alex in playful mood was irresistible. In the bright light of day his way of making love was a light-hearted process, and great fun—until heat and need took over and rocketed them to orgasm in each other's arms. After that there was another shower, and the morning was half gone before they got dressed to sit down to toast prepared by Alex, and eggs scrambled by Sarah.

'Teamwork,' he said with satisfaction. 'You do good eggs.'

'I'm not bad in the kitchen!'

Alex's eyes gleamed. 'Not bad in the bedroom, either.'

'Is that all you can think about?'

He forked in more eggs before replying. 'You're here, in my house, across the table from me eating breakfast, after a night no mere words can describe, so of course I'm thinking about it. I'll probably be thinking about it all week while I'm in endless meetings.'

Sarah smiled and blew him a kiss. 'I'll probably be thinking about it, too, while I get on with the Westhope barns.'

Alex reached out a hand to touch hers. 'Don't expend all your energy on those barns of yours, Sarah. Leave some for evenings with me.'

Sarah was more than happy to do this for the following fortnight, which was a period of marking time for her until the permits came through to start on the barns. Some clearing work in them was all that was possible, and since Ian was now helping them this took very little energy on her part or Harry's.

For Alex certain social commitments were unavoidable some evenings, but they spent the others together at his house—most of them in bed. But Sarah always drove back to Medlar House, and in spite of Alex's persuasion refused to stay overnight at Glebe Barn.

'I'll be happy—deliriously so—to sleep here at weekends,' she promised. 'But because Harry picks me up every morning I'd rather keep to the usual routine during the week.'

Alex eyed her sardonically. 'You don't want him to know about us?'

'Lord, no,' she said, grinning. 'Can you really picture me telling Harry Sollers that my new friend is the vice-chairman of the Merrick Group?'

There was no answering smile from Alex. 'Is that what I am? Your friend?'

She bit her lip, flushing. 'A very special friend. But I can't tell Harry that, either.'

'Why the hell not?'

'Because it's too private to talk about to anyone,' she said, and kissed him so passionately he stopped arguing and made love instead of war.

They spent the weekends in much the same way as the first one. Sarah was now so much at home at Glebe Barn that it was a huge effort to leave it to go back to her flat on Monday mornings, and one particular Monday was worse than usual, because Alex was going away for a while.

'I'm in London, at a conference on global recycling,' he said morosely.

'Just as well,' said Sarah cheerfully. 'Bob has said we can start on the foundations this week, even though the deal isn't final, and when I'm working flat out on that kind of thing I'm tired by the evening most days. And Westhope is a twenty-mile drive for me, instead of just five minutes away like the cottages.'

He nodded moodily. 'I wish you had a less demanding job, Sarah.'

She busied herself with pouring coffee and buttering toast. 'But I don't, so from now on I'll be much better company if we just see each other at weekends. Why the smile?' she added suspiciously.

'Out of all these droves of women apparently languishing for me—or at least my money—I have to fall for the one who doesn't have enough time to fit me into her schedule,' Alex said sardonically. 'I'd begun to hope our relationship meant something to you.'

'It does,' she said, and eyed him warily. 'I'm just not sure what you expect of it, Alex.'

'A hell of a sight more than you're prepared to give,' he snapped, and jumped up to stalk round the table.

She put out her hands to fend him off. 'So tell me what you want.'

'Wasn't last night—and this morning—explanation enough?' He pulled her to her feet. 'You know damn well what I want.'

'Alex, don't rush me,' she said urgently. 'I've only just got used to the idea of you as a friend.'

'Even as a mere friend I'd expect to see more of you than the odd weekend!'

Sarah gazed at him in appeal. 'Once I get the job off the ground at Westhope things will settle down enough for us to see more of each other than that.'

'How generous of you.' Alex stood back, shaking his head in mock wonder. 'I never learn, do I? I should have remembered from past experience of your sex that priorities for a man are not necessarily the same for a woman. Like a fool, I thought you cared for me, Sarah.'

'I *do*.' Sarah blinked hard. 'Surely after what's happened between us you must know that?' She flushed miserably. 'But to strip this down to basics I'm not used to—to this kind of thing on top of a working day. I get tired.'

'By "this kind of thing" you mean sex?' he asked brutally.

The word struck her like a physical blow. 'It's not the word I would have used, but, yes, I suppose that's what I do mean.'

'For me it was a great deal more than that,' he said harshly.

'It was for me, too.'

'But still not enough to combine it with your busy schedule? Or is there something you're not telling me, Sarah?'

She frowned. 'What do you mean?'

His eyes stabbed hers. 'Perhaps you need time away from me to pursue other interests during the week? That's the way it usually goes when a woman pleads for time to herself.'

She stared at him, incensed. 'If you mean seeing another man, it may be usual with the women you know, but it certainly isn't for me!'

'If you say so.' Alex raised a cynical eyebrow. 'But even if your excuses—'

'Reasons, not excuses,' she said hotly.

'Reasons, excuses—it makes no difference. Do you honestly expect me to hang around waiting for whatever crumbs of your company you can spare from your project?'

Sarah looked at him in disbelief. 'If that's the way you feel, no, I don't,' she said, after a tense pause. 'No hanging around expected.'

'Or required!'

'I didn't say that.'

He shrugged. 'It's how it came across.'

Sarah took in a deep breath. 'Talking hypothetically—'

'By all means let's do that!'

She hung on to her temper with difficulty. 'All right. Would you put your London trip off to spend more time with me?'

His shook his head impatiently. 'That's different.'

'Why? Because you're the vice-chairman of the Merrick Group and I'm just an amateur, one-horse property developer— and a female at that?' she demanded.

'Hell and damnation, Sarah, you know I don't think of you

like that.' The sudden burst of heat vanished from his eyes, leaving ice in its place. 'Besides,' he drawled, 'I was merely requesting some of your leisure time, not your hand in marriage.'

She stared at him in disbelief, feeling the colour drain from her face. 'Right,' she said, when she could speak. 'I think that's my cue to leave. Goodbye, Alex.'

Instead of sweeping her into his arms, as she'd half hoped, he nodded formally and carried her overnight bag out to the car.

'Good luck with the barns,' he said distantly, as she got behind the wheel.

Sarah took a last look at his house, then nodded glacially. 'Thank you.'

'Goodbye, Sarah.' Alex walked down to the gate to open it for her, waited as she drove through into the lane, then added the crowning touch to her day by walking straight into the house instead of watching her out of sight.

During her working days she was able to push it from her mind, but in the evenings Sarah seethed constantly over Alex Merrick's parting shot. And sometimes regretted laying down rules about how often they saw each other. But deep down she knew her problem was his typical male assumption that now she'd begun sharing his bed she would be happy to drop everything, any time, to do it again. Presumably whenever he had a moment to spare from the demands of his far more illustrious job, no matter how involved she was with hers.

She shrugged. It was her own fault for getting entangled with someone who was not only used to women flinging themselves at him, but who had once had a relationship with one of them that gave him a jaundiced view of her entire sex. Sarah ground her teeth as his taunt about marriage came back to haunt her, and wished passionately she'd had a cutting riposte to hurl back at him. Instead she'd just walked out. Which was probably as good a response as any.

* * *

When her doorbell rang as she was clearing up after a belated supper one evening, Sarah's heart jumped hopefully to her throat, then sank like a stone in disappointment when she heard Dan Mason's voice over the intercom.

'Could I see you for a moment, Sarah?'

'What do you want?'

'To apologise.'

With reluctance she pressed the buzzer, then opened her door as Dan crossed the hall, looking far from certain of his reception, she noted with satisfaction. 'You'd better come in,' she said coolly.

'Thank you,' he said, with such humility she eyed him in suspicion as she waved him to the sofa.

'So what's brought you down to these parts again, Dan?' she demanded.

'My mother's birthday. But I'm glad of the chance to apologise to you for my behaviour last time I was here.' He fixed her with persuasive blue eyes. 'I was out of order. I'm sorry.'

She shrugged indifferently. 'Apology accepted.'

'Good.' He looked down at his expensive shoes for a moment. 'Word has it you don't patronise the family hostelry these days.'

'No. The project we're working on is a bit far away to pop back for lunch.'

'How about your evenings?' He looked up. 'I know you've been seeing something of Alex Merrick, according to the Green Man grapevine. Is that still on?'

'I'm too busy to see anyone these days,' she said elliptically. 'The barn conversions we're working on leave me too tired to socialise at the end of a working day.'

'Surely you must want a night out now and then?'

'Not really. I get home fit for nothing more than a shower, supper in front of the television, then early bed.'

'That's not much of a life, Sarah!'

'It suits *me*, Dan,' she assured him.

He leaned forward, his eyes suddenly urgent. 'Now you've accepted my apology let me take you out somewhere tomorrow evening. Or if you're not up to going out I could order something in to eat here—'

'No thanks, Dan,' she interrupted. 'I'm not good company right now.'

His eyes hardened. 'Because Merrick dumped you?'

God grant me patience, thought Sarah. 'My private life is my business, Dan.'

He regrouped hurriedly, and gave her a cajoling smile. 'I just want an hour or two with you, Sarah. We spent a pleasant evening together before. Let's do it again.'

Sarah got up. 'Thanks a lot, Dan, but—'

'But you can't. Or won't,' he said bitterly, and jumped up. 'I suppose you're still hankering after Alex Merrick, like all the others before you? I did warn you about him, remember?'

'So you did,' she said wearily, and walked to the door. 'Goodnight, Dan. Drive carefully.'

He paused in the open doorway. 'If you are carrying a torch for Merrick, Sarah, remember what I said. You're a very small fish in your line of business, and he's a great big shark.'

Thoroughly put out by Dan Mason's parting shot, Sarah blanked it out by immersing herself in the back-breaking work of sorting out the floors in the barns. Not even to herself would she admit she was still nourishing the faint hope of a phone call that never happened.

When her phone finally did ring one evening towards the end of the week, she grabbed it eagerly. 'Oh—hi, Harry. What can I do for you?'

'All right if I come round for a minute?'

'Of course. See you soon.' With a sinking feeling Sarah snapped the phone shut. Harry had sounded grim.

When she let him in a few minutes later he looked even grimmer than he'd sounded. 'Come and sit down and tell me what's wrong.' She took her usual place on the windowseat, and waved Harry to the sofa.

'Bob rang me tonight,' he said heavily, his hands clasped between his knees. 'He said I wasn't to tell you, but I think you should know.'

She eyed him in alarm. 'Is there something wrong with the barns?'

'No, not that. But Bob got another offer for them today. Quite a bit more than you've offered for them.' Harry looked her in the eye. 'That's why he didn't want to tell you—in case you thought he was trying to get more money out of you. Bob said it was a young chap called Harris who called on him to make the offer. Ever heard of him?'

Sarah sat stunned for a moment. 'Oh, yes, I've heard of him,' she said at last. 'He works for Alex Merrick.'

Harry stared. 'Does he, by God? I didn't know that. Bob neither. Tall young fellow with glasses, he said.'

'That's the one.' Her eyes kindled. 'But I seriously doubt that Greg Harris is going into barn conversion on his own.'

Harry grimaced. 'Mavis was blazing. Everything about to be signed and sealed, she reminded Bob, and besides, she'd already spent some of Miss Carver's deposit on the baby. Bob said they had a right old set-to before he could shut her up long enough to say he had no intention of accepting the offer—'

Sarah tried to smile. 'It must be a bit galling for him to know he could have got more money for them, though.'

'Bob's one of the old school,' said Harry, getting up. He'd given his word. As far as he's concerned that's that.' He gave Sarah a searching look. 'Don't worry about it. Have a good sleep and I'll call for you in the morning.'

'Thanks, Harry. But you and Ian take tomorrow off. I'm going to sort this out.' She smiled at him. 'Thanks for coming round.'

'Sorry I brought bad news,' he said gruffly.

She shrugged. 'I had to know.'

Sarah saw Harry off, then booted up her laptop and wrote a short, very explicit letter to Alex Merrick, printed it, and signed it with a flourish. She printed out an envelope, folded the letter into it and put it in her handbag, then lay in a warm bath until she felt calm enough to go to bed.

At ten next morning Sarah parked in front of the Merrick office building and walked into the foyer to confront the receptionist.

'Sarah Carver,' she said crisply. 'I'd like to see Mr Alex Merrick, please. I don't have an appointment.'

The woman smiled politely. 'I'll see if he's available.'

Sarah felt a surge of triumph. At least he was here in the building.

'Mr Merrick is in a meeting, but he'll see you in fifteen minutes, if you care to wait, Miss Carver,' said the receptionist, putting the phone down.

'Thanks.' Sarah took a seat on one of the leather chesterfields, and stared blindly at a magazine until the receptionist came to tell her Mr Merrick was free.

Alex had wound up his meeting sooner than intended, then sprinted to his office to sit behind his desk, all kinds of reasons for Sarah's visit chasing through his brain as he waited for her to appear. It was unlikely she was coming here to his office to mend things between them. Though he hoped to God she had. The knock on the door brought him upright in his seat, but his voice was calm as he bade her come in.

Last time she'd been here, to sign the deal on the cottages, Sarah had been a vision in some kind of dark red, but today she wore a severe black suit. Her hair was dragged back into a ruthless knot and her mood, he saw at a glance, matched the suit.

'Good morning,' he said, rising. 'This is a surprise.'

'Good morning. It's good of you to spare the time to see me.'

'For God's sake, Sarah,' he said wearily. 'Of course I've got time to see you. What's wrong?'

'Why should anything be wrong?' she countered. 'I came to deliver a letter, in case you were away, but since I'm lucky enough to speak to you face to face I won't bother with that.'

'Please sit down, Sarah,' said Alex.

'Thank you, I'd rather stand.'

'Sit down,' he repeated, without raising his voice.

'As you wish,' she said, shrugging, and took the chair facing him.

'Now, tell me why you're here.'

'To tell you I think you're despicable,' she said coldly.

The steady eyes didn't so much as flicker. 'Despicable?' he repeated, and raised an eyebrow. 'Would you care to expand on that? We crossed swords over my desire to see more of you. You didn't want that. What, exactly, is so despicable? Should I have been more persistent?'

'Oh, stop tap-dancing, Alex,' she said wearily. 'You know exactly why I'm here. You topped my offer to Bob Grover for his barns.'

Alex stared at her, no vestige of expression on his face. 'No, Sarah,' he said, after a silence so long she was ready to scream, 'I most certainly did not.'

'Oh, all right, if you must split hairs. It was Greg Harris who made the offer.'

'What the hell would Greg Harris want with the barns?'

'He doesn't want them. You know perfectly well he was acting on your behalf,' she snapped. 'You couldn't take it when I preferred to work on them rather than see more of you. So to massage your damaged ego you put a spoke in my wheel in true Merrick fashion. You won't have any luck, though. Bob Grover won't go back on his word to me.'

Alex subjected her to another fraught silence, then picked up his phone. 'Come in, please.'

Greg Harris greeted Sarah politely, and looked at his employer in enquiry.

'Have you ever been to Westhope Farm?' asked Alex.

The young man thought for a moment. 'No. I don't even know where it is.'

'Are you sure? It's about fifteen miles the other side of Hereford.'

Greg shook his head. 'Sorry, Alex. Do you want some information on it?'

'No. I want you to go there with me, right now. Postpone the rest of my morning appointments, contact Mr Grover at Westhope Farm to make sure he's free, then meet me down in the car park.'

When the young man had gone, Sarah got up. 'I've had enough of this charade. I'm leaving—'

'No, Sarah,' rapped Alex, in a tone so hard it startled her. 'You started this. You're coming to Westhope Farm to see it through.'

'I most certainly am not!'

'Why? Are you afraid you'll be proved wrong?' he asked, with a smile which made her clench her fists. 'I wouldn't have put you down as a coward, Sarah.'

She glared at him, but Alex stood up, his eyes ice-cold as they held hers, and at last, to her mortification, hers were the first to fall. 'Oh, very well,' she said ungraciously. 'I'll follow you in my car.'

'Oh, no! You travel in mine.' Alex held the office door open for her, and Sarah walked out to the lift in stony silence.

To Sarah's chagrin she was shown into the back seat of the Cherokee, and virtually ignored while Alex chatted to Greg in front. The only time he spoke directly to her was to ask directions to the farm when they left the Leominster road.

'I'm sure you know exactly where it is,' she said tartly, though by this time tendrils of doubt were beginning to creep up on her.

'It's years since I've been out this way, so I don't remember precisely,' he said, and told Greg to consult the map. 'Since Miss Carver is uncooperative, we'll blunder on the best we can.'

When they'd passed the turning down to Westhope and driven a mile further on Sarah gave up.

'Go back and take the next left,' she snapped. 'As you well know.'

Greg, she saw with satisfaction, looked hideously uncomfortable, which scotched any doubts she'd been feeling. He was very obviously not looking forward to an encounter with Bob Grover.

When they finally drove past the trio of barns to arrive at the farm, Alex surprised Sarah by staying in the car.

'Greg will go to the door with you,' he said.

'What am I supposed to ask, Alex?' asked his unhappy assistant.

'Just to see Mr Grover. I'm sure Miss Carver will take it from there.'

Greg opened the Jeep door to a chorus of barking, and helped Sarah down. He took out a handkerchief to wipe his glasses and then settled them firmly on his nose, plainly relieved when the stocky figure of Bob Grover appeared, to quiet the dogs.

'Hello there, Sarah,' said Bob, smiling, and looked enquiringly at Greg.

'Good morning. You remember Greg Harris, Mr Grover?' she said. 'Harry told me you've met before. When Mr Harris made you an offer.'

Bob looked at the young man blankly, and shook his head. 'No. This isn't the chap, Sarah.'

'There's obviously been some mistake, Miss Carver,' said Greg stiffly, and turned in relief as Alex came to join them, smiling warmly at the farmer.

'Hello, Mr Grover.'

Bob's weatherbeaten face lit up. 'Alex Merrick? Well, I never. Haven't seen you since you were a nipper. How's old Edgar?'

'In rude health, thanks. Nice to see you again,' said Alex, shaking hands. He cast a cold glance at Sarah. 'Someone's been causing trouble, Mr Grover, by posing as Greg here to make an offer for your barns. I'd like to know who it was.'

'So would I,' said Bob fiercely. 'Come in, the three of you. My wife is out, but I can put the kettle on.'

'That's very kind of you,' said Alex, 'but I'm pushed for time. Could you describe this man for me?'

Bob thought hard. 'He was tall, about your age, and wore a suit and glasses. He drove a fancy foreign car.'

Sarah wanted to dig a hole in the farmyard and bury herself in it as Bob described a yellow Ferrari in detail.

'He'd left it out on a verge, out of sight along the lane,' he explained. 'But it had settled into thickish mud when he went back to it, and he had to ask for help to push it out.'

'Thanks, Mr Grover,' said Alex. 'Mystery solved. An old schoolfriend of mine playing a practical joke. I'll have words with him.'

'I'd like some words with the idiot myself,' growled Bob. 'It upset Mavis good and proper, I can tell you. Not,' he said, smiling at Sarah, 'that it made any difference. Miss Carver knows she can trust me to keep my word.'

'I do indeed, Mr Grover,' she assured him.

'Trust is a very valuable commodity,' said Alex pointedly. 'Good to see you again, Mr Grover.'

'Give your grandfather my regards.' Bob turned to Sarah. 'You'll be here in the morning, then?'

'That's right. Tell your wife I'm sorry I missed her.' Sarah managed a smile for him, then walked to the Cherokee, feeling like Marie Antoinette on the way to the guillotine.

Alex motioned to Greg to get in the car, but barred Sarah's way.

'What the hell was your boyfriend playing at?' he asked in a furious undertone.

'Boyfriend?' Sarah eyed him balefully. 'You know perfectly well that Dan Mason is not, and never has been, my "boyfriend".'

'Then what was he doing at your place the other night?'

'How do you know he was there?' she asked involuntarily.

'I was idiot enough to call to see you,' said Alex with disgust.

'But I saw the Ferrari parked outside Medlar House and thought better of it."

Sarah could have cried. 'Dan came to apologise for his behavious and to ask me out again. I refused the offer. End of story.'

'Do you mean the bastard made that offer to Bob Groves as a form of revenge? It certainly worked—on both of us.' He gave her a look which made her quail. 'Did you really believe I would do something so petty, Sarah? Don't bother to answer,' he added harshly. 'You obviously did. Please get in the car.'

In embarrassed silence Greg Harris helped her into the back, then got in beside Alex, which left her no opportunity to apologise on the endless journey back. By the time they reached the Merrick building Sarah was word-perfect in various speeches, but when Alex parked the Cherokee it was Greg who came to hand her out, and no speeches were necessary.

'I've wasted enough time this morning,' Alex said, looking at his watch. 'See Miss Carver to her car, Greg.' And, without even a look in Sarah's direction, the vice-chairman of the Merrick Group strode inside to rule his kingdom, leaving his assistant to carry out his orders with body language which made his opinion of the morning's fiasco very plain.

Sarah burned with humiliation on the drive home. But gradually it gave way to a cold feeling of loss. One thing was clear. She would have all the time in the world to concentrate on the Westhope job. Alex would never want to set eyes on her again. She'd paid him back well and truly for his jibe about marriage. As she thought of her crack about his ego she shivered, seized by a burning desire to black both of Dan Mason's lying blue eyes.

'Bob told me what happened,' said Harry on the phone later. 'Fancy some lunch at the pub?'

'Oh, yes, please,' said Sarah fervently.

'Right. I'll pick you up in five minutes.'

On the way Sarah gave Harry a detailed account of her morning, and sighed heavily as he drew up outside the Green

Man. 'A good job I'm not in Oliver's line of work. I accused Alex Merrick without a shred of actual proof that he was behind the offer.'

'But why would you think *he* wanted the barns?' said Harry, frowning. 'The Merricks don't do small stuff like that any more. It was different with the cottages. They were next to the hotel site.'

'I've been seeing something of Alex lately—socially, I mean,' said Sarah reluctantly. 'But we had a row.'

Harry's shrewd blue eyes met hers. 'Must have been some row if you thought he'd tried to queer your pitch with Bob.'

'It was.' She smiled brightly. 'But after the insults I hurled at him this morning he'll never want to lay eyes on me again, so my social time is all mine again.'

'Learn to play darts,' advised Harry, as they went into the pub. 'You can play with Fred and me of an evening some time.'

'I used to play a bit,' she assured him. 'In my building site days I wasn't bad.'

'Hear that?' said Harry, as Fred joined them. 'The lady says she's good with the arrows.'

Sarah felt so much better by the time she'd eaten a sandwich and downed some cider that it didn't take much persuasion when Fred fetched some darts and challenged her to a game. She took off her jacket, rolled up the sleeves of her white shirt, projected a mental image of Dan Mason's face on the board, and did so well with her first few throws that a small crowd gathered to watch.

By the time she was well on the way to beating Fred at his own game, Sarah's hair was beginning to unravel from its knot, and she'd kicked off her high heels. She let out a crow of triumph as she beat him with her last throw. When a cheer went up from the onlookers she turned to bow all round, then blushed to the roots of her hair at the sight of Alex at the other end of the bar, talking to Eddy Mason. He nodded coldly, and for the second time that day Sarah wanted to run and hide. She returned the nod, thrust her feet into her shoes, and stood between Fred and Harry, forcing herself to finish her drink before looking in Alex's direction again. And found he'd gone.

CHAPTER ELEVEN

SARAH HAD been so sure Alex had come to the Green Man to look for her she was utterly devastated when he left without a word. Message received, loud and clear, she thought miserably. Even so, she still had to apologise. If she rang him there was every likelihood that he'd refuse to speak to her, so the only option was a letter. But when she'd finished it, the typewritten letter seemed too cold for an apology. With a sigh she copied it in longhand, and then went out to post it before she could change her mind. It had been incredibly difficult to express herself in a way which apologised for her accusations and at the same tried to hint that a reply would be welcome.

When no reply arrived Sarah faced the truth. It was time to forget Alex Merrick, along with fancy underwear and dresses with sequins. Life from now on would consist of overalls, a hard hat, and hard work.

Sarah was grateful to get back to hard labour with Harry and Ian at Westhope next day. In the beginning, because they were too far away for pub lunches at the Green Man, all three of them had taken sandwiches, but Mavis Grover, shocked at the thought of them functioning all day on such meagre fuel, had insisted that she would make lunch for them. Since she was Harry's sister and Ian's aunt, Sarah had had no choice but to accept— but only, she'd said firmly, if Mavis accepted payment. Also, the lunch must be something simple and easy to eat during their break in one of the barns, instead of at Mavis's table. After seeing the state of all three of them halfway through the first day's work Mavis had given in on this, but beaten Sarah down on the sum she considered fair in return for a few snacks.

The arrangement meant that Sarah ate something nourishing at least once a day—which was a good thing, she conceded wearily, when she was too tired to do more than open a tin or make a sandwich after Harry dropped her off each night.

Fred drove to visit them on site a few days later, to tell them Daniel Mason had been mugged outside his London flat. According to his father he'd been lucky to come out of it with nothing worse than a black eye.

'Betty Mason is pretty upset about it,' reported Fred, over a hunk of the steak and ale pie Mavis had insisted he stay to share.

Sarah plumbed a dark side of herself she hadn't known existed as she tried not to rejoice at the news. Her only regret was not blacking Dan's eye herself.

'Serves him right for that trick he tried to play on Sarah and Bob,' said Harry, and gave Ian the details.

'If I'd known about it,' said his large nephew, clenching formidable fists, 'I'd have beaten him up before he ever got back to London.'

'Best you kept out of it, lad,' said Harry.

Sarah broke off a piece of piecrust for Nero. 'Did Dan have much stolen from him?'

Fred shook his head. 'Nothing at all. A crowd of thugs just jumped him for the pleasure of it, seemingly.'

Good for them, thought Sarah fervently.

During one of Oliver's weekend phone calls he suggested coming down to take her out to lunch one Sunday soon. 'I shall put up at the Green Dragon overnight, as usual, and drive back first thing on Monday morning. How about the restaurant we went to with Alex Merrick? What was it called?'

'The Pheasant.'

'That's the one. Good food there; decent wine list, too. You can bring me up to speed on your progress.'

Speed was hardly the word. Securing and relaying the floors was hard, slow work, and Harry admitted he was as grateful as she was for Ian's tireless help. Once that stage was over a footing inspection would be necessary before they could go any further. But by the time Oliver arrived on the appointed weekend, attired in a tweed suit of impeccable pedigree, Sarah reported that once Harry had treated all the wood they would be ready to start on the roofs before they went on to the next step of lining the walls with quick-drying membrane to render them waterproof.

'You look tired, darling,' said Oliver, as he drove her to the Pheasant.

'I've been working hard.'

'You never do anything else.' He shook his head in disapproval. 'It seems entirely wrong for a girl of your age.'

'I enjoy it, Oliver. And this time it's easier because I have Harry's nephew Ian working for me on a permanent basis.' Sarah patted his solid, tweed-clad knee. 'Stop worrying about me. Let's just enjoy our lunch.'

They were welcomed at the door by a smartly dressed redhead Sarah took to be Jane Hicks, Stephen's wife. She showed them into one of the smaller dining rooms, and seated them with a view of the pretty garden at the back of the pub.

'We do Sunday roasts of varying kinds, but you can order from the *à la carte* menu if you prefer.' She handed out menus, gave Oliver the wine list, and with a smile excused herself to see to the next arrivals.

Once a waiter had taken their order for wine, Oliver sat back to peruse the menu with his customary respect for the business of eating.

'Good place, this,' he commented, as he ran his eye down the list of choices. 'I'm torn between the rack of lamb and the roast duck.'

Sarah smiled at him fondly. 'Not your usual steak today?'

'For once, no. I'll keep to Sunday lunch convention.' Oliver was presented with a bottle of wine to inspect. A little was poured into his glass, he tasted, rolled it round his palate, then nodded in approval, and the waiter filled their glasses.

Well used to the ritual, Sarah went on studying the menu, then looked up with interest when a feminine voice said, 'Oliver Moore! How are you?'

Oliver rose to his feet with a delighted smile. 'Helen! How wonderful to see you.'

'Likewise.' The lady was tall, with stylishly cut fair hair and large hazel eyes which smiled at Sarah in enquiry. 'Hello. I'm Helen Alexander.'

'This is my goddaughter, Sarah Carver,' said Oliver, and pulled out a chair. 'Do join us.'

'I'd love to, my dear, but I'm lunching in the next room with my sister-in-law and my son. Our meal will soon be ready, so I must get back. All right, Alex—I'm coming,' she added, as an all too familiar figure joined her. 'Look who's here, darling.'

'Hello, Sarah,' said Alex briefly, and shook hands with Oliver. 'How are you, sir?'

'Very well, my boy,' said Oliver. 'I liked the place so much the day you brought us, I persuaded Sarah to eat here again.'

'Stephen's a fabulous chef, isn't he?' said Helen. 'Do you live nearby, Sarah?'

'Yes.' Sarah found her voice at last. 'I have a flat in Medlar House—the old girls' school.'

'Really? It's such a lovely building. I always wanted to look round it, but I didn't have a daughter as a pretext.' Helen smiled at her son. 'Alex knew it well. He went to parties there when he was young.'

'I've heard about the parties,' said Sarah.

'How is your project coming along?' Alex asked her stiffly.

His mother looked at him in surprise. 'You two know each other professionally?'

'Of course they do,' said Oliver. 'Sarah's in the same line of business.'

'Scrap metal?' said Helen, astonished.

Alex shook his head. 'Sarah's involved in property conversions.'

'Then you really must take her to see your barn, darling.'

'She's already seen it,' her son informed her shortly. 'We'd better get back to our table. Aunt Bel will be wondering where we are.'

Helen Alexander offered a cheek to Oliver to kiss, and smiled warmly at Sarah. 'Come and take another look at Alex's house while I'm staying there. I'll give you tea.'

'Sarah's far too busy to waste time on mere socialising,' said Alex coldly, and won a look of shocked disapproval from his parent.

'Perhaps you'd have tea with me at Medlar House instead, Mrs Alexander?' said Sarah, surprising him. And herself. 'I never work on Sundays.'

'Why, thank you. I'd like that very much indeed. Next week?' said Helen, ignoring her son's stony face. 'I leave for home shortly after that.'

Oliver regarded Sarah with intense interest when they were alone. 'Did I detect a certain *froideur* between you and young Merrick?'

'Yes,' said Sarah baldly, and turned away in relief as a waitress came to take their order.

A past-master at cross-examination, Oliver returned to the subject as soon as they were alone. 'The last time we were here I gained the distinct impression that young Alex was smitten with you.'

'You were wrong,' she said flatly. 'Do you know his mother well?'

'I met her at some party, back in the mists of time. Like a fool I introduced her to George Merrick and lost her to the younger man.' Oliver looked down his formidable nose. 'But now he's lost Helen, which makes *him* the fool.'

The encounter with Alex's attractive mother made Sarah deeply curious to know more. 'Why did she leave him?'

'Usual story—another woman. Stupid idiot,' Oliver added bitterly.

'Cheer up,' said Sarah, as much to herself as to Oliver. 'Here comes our lunch.'

Much as she would have liked to eat and run, to avoid seeing Alex again, Sarah knew from experience that Oliver refused to be rushed when it came to food. And since in this case it was excellent, she did her best to enjoy it while she described her current work on the barns.

'No wonder you're looking thinner,' said Oliver with disapproval. 'Do you cook for yourself when you get home at night?'

'I don't have to. Mrs Grover cooks for the three of us at lunchtime.' Sarah explained the catering arrangement. 'Now, tell me about your latest case. Have you been defending anyone famous?'

While Oliver enjoyed his usual ripe Stilton, Sarah pushed some ice cream round a dish, but put her spoon down when Helen Alexander came back with another woman in tow.

'Miss Merrick,' said Oliver, rising to his feet. 'How good to see you. Let me introduce you to my goddaughter, Sarah Carver.'

Isabel Merrick turned familiar grey eyes on Sarah. 'How do you do, my dear? Helen tells me you're in the same line of business as my family.'

Sarah smiled. 'On a very much smaller scale.'

'What have you done with Edgar today?' asked Oliver.

'Our invaluable housekeeper is giving Father his lunch to let me off for an hour or two,' said Bel Merrick, rolling her eyes. 'But I'd better be back in good time for his afternoon tea.'

'I'll do that today,' said Helen firmly. 'You shouldn't let him ride roughshod over you, Bel.'

'You mustn't bore Miss Carver with our family secrets, Mother,' interrupted Alex as he joined them.

'Old Edgar's tyranny is no secret,' said Oliver wryly.

'Very true,' agreed Helen. 'It keeps him alive. Are you staying the night with Sarah, Oliver?'

'No room at her place, m'dear. I'm in my usual berth at the Green Dragon in Hereford.'

'A favourite haunt of yours, I seem to remember.' She turned to Sarah. 'Next Sunday at about four, then?'

Sarah smiled warmly. 'I'll look forward to it.'

In the general chorus of goodbyes Sarah and Alex pointedly ignored each other—something duly noted by Oliver once they were alone.

'Daggers drawn, obviously,' he said, beckoning to a waitress. 'Have some coffee and tell me why the electricity positively crackles between you and young Alex.'

'We had a disagreement over something trivial,' she said flatly, and changed the subject.

The encounter with Alex gave Sarah such a restless night that Harry eyed her warily when he picked her up next morning.

'Bad head?'

'Bad night.' She tapped her Thermos of coffee. 'A couple more cups of this and I'll be fine.' She explained about Oliver's visit. 'I ate too much lunch yesterday.'

'Not something you do any other day,' he said sharply. 'Don't think I haven't noticed.'

'Your sister always gives me too much,' she protested.

'You give half of it to Nero most times. What are you fretting about, boss? Is it the job?'

'No, Harry. I love the work.' She shrugged. 'But, as you know by now, some days I feel a bit down.'

'When you miss your father?'

'Yes,' she said, which was only half the truth. The other half was Alex Merrick's fault. She'd persuaded herself she was getting over him. But one look at him yesterday had made it clear that wasn't going to happen any time soon. Her mouth set. She'd get there in the end.

Sarah was glad when Friday arrived, and she had two days off to look forward to.

'Will you be wanting me on Saturday this week, boss?' asked Ian as they were packing up.

'No. We're well on schedule,' she said, patting Nero. 'I need tomorrow off for stocking up on food—'

'And eating some of it,' muttered Harry.

'For heaven's sake, stop *nagging* me—' She took in a deep breath. 'Sorry—sorry! I'm a bit tired—which is no excuse for shouting at you, Harry.'

'Let's get you home,' he said gruffly. 'It's been a long day.'

Sarah was glad, not for the first time, that she wasn't driving on the way back. Harry had suggested he took on this job from day one, and after insisting she paid for petrol Sarah had been only too happy to agree.

'You can rip at me again if you like,' he said, once they were underway, 'but you'd do well to stay in bed for a bit in the morning before you do that shopping.'

'I certainly will. I'm looking forward to it,' she agreed, yawning. 'But cleaning comes before shopping. Not the windows,' she added hastily. 'They still look fine.'

Harry's lips twitched. 'I'm not offering to do that lot again in a hurry. Not after the day we've had, that's for sure.'

'That's the trouble with our kind of work,' said Sarah with a sigh. 'It doesn't leave much energy over for going out in the evenings.' Which only proved the point she'd tried to make to Alex. Though if he could see her right now, she thought bitterly, her face grey with fatigue and her hair stuck to her head with sweat, he'd run for his life, offering up thanks for his escape.

By half past three on Sunday afternoon, Sarah was beginning to regret her impulsive invitation to Alex's mother. In part, Sarah knew only too well, it had been a knee-jerk response to his sarcastic crack about her social time. Or lack of it. But there was something about Helen Alexander as a person which called strongly to Sarah, and made her eager to know her better.

So now her flat was shining, she'd arranged flowers at one end of her trestle table, and set a tea tray ready in the kitchen. She'd taken extra care with her hair and face, and wore a pink cotton shirt tucked into the white jeans of her night with Alex. Since it was no use even for an evening with Oliver, the sequinned dress was bundled up in a bag, ready for a charity shop next time she was in Hereford. Her lips twitched as she thought of Oliver's reaction to the dress. Oliver liked to think of himself as broad-minded, but not, she had a fair idea, when it came to his goddaughter.

When Sarah's bell rang promptly at four, she pressed the buzzer for the outer door, then walked across the hall to greet Alex's mother. 'Welcome to my retreat,' she said, smiling as she led the way back to the flat.

Helen Alexander, cool and attractive in a leaf green linen dress, greeted her warmly. But when Sarah ushered her inside the beautiful hazel eyes widened in awe as Helen took in the dimensions of the room. 'My dear girl,' she said, impressed. 'What a wonderful retreat it is. Alex told me it's all your own work, that you actually fitted it up yourself, so show me exactly what you've done.'

In the face of such genuine interest Sarah found herself giving every detail, but at last apologised for going on too long and offered her visitor tea. 'I won't be a moment. My kitchen's a bit small, Mrs Alexander—'

'It's Miss these days,' her visitor corrected, as she followed her to the kitchen doorway. 'I reverted to my maiden name after my divorce. But just Helen will do.'

'Thank you.' Sarah smiled in apology as she poured boiling water on to teabags in her best cups. 'I'm afraid that, unlike Alex, I don't have a teapot. At least not here with me. That kind of thing is still in store in London. But the cups were my mother's.'

Helen eyed her speculatively. 'Sarah, I normally scoff at women who talk about their intuition, but even Bel noticed something in the air between you and Alex. And if you're acquainted with his teapot you must know him quite well.'

Sarah picked up the tray. 'He bought the cottages I restored.'

'He showed them to me. I was deeply impressed.' The hazel eyes were searching. 'But if you've been to his house there's a lot more to it than that. Alex tends to keep his home off limits to visitors.'

'We met occasionally in the run-up to the sale of the cottages, and we've had dinner together a couple of times since,' Sarah said casually, and carried the tray over to the table. 'Would you like some cake? Home made—though by the lady who bakes for the local Post Office stores, not by me.'

'Honest creature! I'd love a piece of cake.' Helen took it, and sat down in the cherrywood rocker. 'So, tell me about yourself, Sarah. I know you're Oliver Moore's goddaughter.'

Sarah explained about the relationship. 'He was always a hands-on godfather, but since Dad died Oliver takes his duties even more seriously.' She smiled wryly. 'My way of earning a living gives him nightmares. Irregular income, plus down-and-dirty physical labour.'

Helen looked thoughtful as she ate some cake. 'Oliver would rather you worked office hours in a pretty dress?'

Sarah grinned. 'Exactly. But that's enough about me. Alex said you live in Stratford? You enjoy that?'

'I do—very much. I bought a flat near my sister, and I've made quite a lot of friends there, not to mention having the Royal Shakespeare Theatre on hand.' Helen smiled wryly. 'It's not too far from London, or to visit Alex—and Bel and old Edgar, of course. After my divorce I wanted to go abroad as far as I could get at first, but I soon got over that. I need to be at least in the same country as my son. Though not near enough,' she added with a smile, 'to be breathing down his neck.'

'From the way Alex talks about you, that's not a problem for him.'

'Does he talk about me?'

'Not in detail. He told me about your visits.' Sarah hesitated. 'He doesn't resemble you at all physically.'

Helen smiled ruefully. 'No. He's his father all over again. When I first met George he looked very much as Alex does now. Perhaps you can understand why I was swept off my feet?'

'Yes, I can,' said Sarah bleakly. 'Alex is a very attractive man.'

'And it's obvious that he thinks the same about you,' said Helen gently. 'So what went wrong?'

Sarah looked into the sympathetic eyes for a moment, then found herself pouring out the entire story—from her initial aversion to the mere name of Merrick, to the hideously embarrassing scene with Bob Grover at Westhope Farm. 'I wrote to Alex to apologise,' she finished forlornly, 'but no reply. And by his attitude the other day at the Pheasant I'm not likely to get one. Not,' she added hastily, 'that I blame him. But I still think he was unreasonable in some ways.'

'And what ways were they?'

'I get pretty tired during the week when I'm working flat-out, so I suggested—no, pleaded with him,' she added bitterly, 'to save our time together for weekends.'

'And of course Alex, typical male that he is—and a Merrick at that—thought he should see you whenever he wanted to,' said Helen, nodding. 'So you took it for granted he was the one who did the stunt at Westhope Farm in petty revenge?'

Sarah flushed hectically. 'I can't believe, now, that I made such a terrible mistake without checking it out.'

'But in spite of all this you still like my son?'

'Much too much for my peace of mind. But don't tell him that,' Sarah added hastily.

'Of course not.' Helen got up. 'How about some more tea while I tell you something which may help you to understand Alex better?' She handed the cake plate over. 'I should put the rest of that in a tin right away, so it doesn't dry.'

When they were back in their former places, holding fresh cups of tea, Helen gave Sarah an odd little smile. 'Tell me if

I'm imagining things, but do you share this rapport I feel between us?'

'I most certainly do,' Sarah assured her. 'It was part of my reason for asking you here.'

Helen chuckled. 'And was the other part due to Alex's rudeness about your lack of social life, by any chance?'

Sarah nodded sheepishly. 'He annoyed me.'

'I could tell! It's obvious that you two have very strong feelings for each other, even if they're not exactly cordial right now. So, be honest with me. Do you love my son?'

Sarah stared at her, startled, her first instinct to deny it vehemently. But the steady hazel eyes were so compelling it was impossible to lie. 'Yes, I do,' she said despondently. 'For all the good it will do me now.'

Helen smiled reassuringly. 'It will, I promise. Because Alex feels the same about you, Sarah. He gives himself away every time I mention your name. So, to understand him you should know that he had a pretty nasty experience at the hands of one young woman. It tends to colour his view of our sex.'

'Which doesn't mean he has to tar me with the same brush, Helen.' Sarah sighed. 'He was totally unreasonable.'

'Of course he was. He's a man! Now, I must go—or Edgar will be giving Bel the third degree about where I've gone. Poor dear, I don't know how she puts up with him. Well, I do, really. She does it because she loves him. So do I, the old tyrant. You should meet him. He'd like you.'

Sarah shook her head as she accompanied her visitor to the door. 'One Merrick was more than enough for me.'

'I have some advice for you,' said Helen. 'You probably won't want to follow it, but I'll give it anyway. Alex will be at home next weekend, because he's doing something to his garden. If you turn up out of the blue I doubt he'll send you away.'

'I can't see myself doing that,' said Sarah ruefully. 'But thanks anyway.'

'By the way,' said Helen, as they walked outside, 'who did cause the mischief with Westhope Farm?'

'A man called Dan Mason. His parents keep the Green Man. Do you know him?'

'I know of him. He was the hugely bright boy who walked away with all the prizes on Speech Day when Alex was in school.' She shook her head in wonder. 'What on earth made him do such a preposterous thing?'

Sarah's mouth turned down. 'It sounds a bit big-headed, but I think it was just to cause trouble because I preferred Alex to him.'

'And are you going to let him get away with it?' said Helen slyly.

Sarah looked into the challenging hazel gaze and came to a decision. 'No. No, I'm not. I'll take your advice and beard the lion in his den next Sunday. Alex can't eat me.'

Helen took two cards from her bag and gave one to Sarah. 'Ring me to tell me how you got on. Ring me any time you want, in fact. Whatever happens with you and Alex, I'd like to keep in touch with you, Sarah. Now, tell me your number and I'll scribble it down. Goodbye, my dear.' Her eyes sparkled. 'Shall I give Alex your love?'

Sarah shook her head. 'I doubt that he'd want it right now.'

'Oh, he would. We mothers know these things,' said Helen, and smiled wickedly as the doorbell rang. 'There he is now, come to drive me home.'

When the bell gave a peremptory second ring, Sarah gave Helen a wild look and picked up the receiver.

'Alex here.' The familiar voice set Sarah's pulse racing. 'Is my mother ready?'

Sarah pressed the button to release the outer door, then opened her own. Helen stood beside her as they watched Alex cross the hall towards them. 'I could have gone outside, but this is so much more interesting,' she whispered.

'Hello, Sarah,' said Alex woodenly as he reached them.

'Hi,' she returned, managing to paste on a smile.

'Thank you for tea, Sarah,' said Helen. 'And for showing me your quite remarkable home. It's amazing, isn't it, Alex?'

'Yes,' he agreed stiffly, then, as if the words were torn from him, 'How are you, Sarah?'

'Absolutely fine,' she lied. 'How are you?'

'I'm absolutely fine, too.' He turned to his mother. 'Are you ready?'

'Yes, dear.' Helen kissed Sarah's cheek. 'Thank you again. I've enjoyed my afternoon. I'm going home tomorrow, so I'll say goodbye. Perhaps you'll give me tea again next time I'm here?'

'I'd be very happy to. Thank you so much for coming.'

Alex gave Sarah a formal nod as he took his mother's arm. Helen turned to wave at the outer door and Sarah waved back, but Alex kept his back turned as he hurried his mother out to the car.

CHAPTER TWELVE

RAIN CAME down in sheets as the Jensen left the courtyard, so instead of a peaceful stroll in the gardens Sarah settled down to the paperwork she'd been too tired to work on during the week. Afterwards she rang Oliver, to report progress and tell him about the visit from Alex's mother.

'Got to go, Oliver,' she said as the doorbell rang. 'Someone's at the door. I'll ring you next week.'

The sound of Alex's voice over the intercom again sent Sarah so haywire her hand shook as she pressed the button to let him in.

He strode across the Sunday quiet of the hall towards her, rain dripping down his shirt from his hair. Without a word he pushed her inside, thrust the door shut behind him, and seized her in his arms, kissing her with a craving she responded to helplessly.

'I can't do this any more,' he said hoarsely, when he raised his head.

'Do—what—?' she gasped.

'I give in. To hell with it. I'll take your terms. Whatever I can get.' His mouth found hers again, and for a hot, breathless interval they kissed with a wildness that left them shaking when she pushed him away far enough to let her look up into his face.

'Let me say I'm sorry, Alex,' she said, in a voice so unsteady it sounded like a stranger's. 'I should have known—'

His kiss smothered the rest of her plea, and for a while it seemed more important to kiss him back than to try and talk.

'No—please,' she panted at last. 'You must let me speak. I should have trusted you. Known you wouldn't do anything so monstrous. I would have apologised as soon as we got back from Westhope, but you didn't give me the chance.'

'Because I was mad as hell,' he said, and kissed her again. 'As soon as I simmered down I went looking for you at Medlar House, but no luck, So I tried the Green Man.' His eyes blazed into hers. 'And there you were, without a care in the world, playing darts, for God's sake.'

'So you stormed off without a word again.' Sarah buried her head against his damp shirtfront. 'It cut me to pieces.'

'It didn't do me much good, either.' He rubbed his cheek over her tangled curls. 'I know the perfect way to put the pieces back together. But there's a snag. We're in the wrong place. My healing process needs a bed.' Alex put a finger under her chin to raise her face to his. 'If I made love to you on your balcony, Juliet, I'd wreck it, the way I feel right now.'

Sarah felt a hot thrill run through her at the mere thought. 'I have a much safer alternative. My windowseat has a secret life. It's really the lid of a storage box.' She ran to raise it and drew out the thick winter duvet stored under it.

Alex's smile lit up the room as he snatched the quilt from her to throw it down on the rug. He held out his arms. 'Then come lie with me, wench, so I can kiss you better.'

'You'd better take that wet shirt off first!'

He smiled his crooked smile. 'I'd rather dispense with yours.'

'You'll have to, if you're going to kiss me better,' she said, her eyes steady on his. 'Because I hurt all over.'

'In that case,' said Alex, eyes glittering, 'you'd better have some cushions, too.' He took some from the windowseat and tossed them down on the quilt, then pulled the blinds closed and drew her down full-length beside him. 'Where shall I start?' he asked, looking down into her eyes.

'The shirt,' she reminded him gruffly.

'Ah, yes.' Alex sat up, undid his shirt and tossed it over his head, then began to undo Sarah's, his lips following his fingers.

'Plain white cotton today,' she said breathlessly, as he flung her shirt to join his. 'I put the fancy stuff away.'

'Why?'

'Not suitable for the kind of work I've been doing.' Sarah bit her lip. 'Besides, I couldn't bear the sight of it any more.'

He frowned. 'You haven't thrown it out?'

'It was too expensive for that.' Her eyes met his. 'But the dress with the sequins is about to go.'

'No way,' he said sternly. 'I have a particular fondness for that dress.' He pulled her close. 'I want you so much, Sarah.'

'Then for heaven's sake do something about it,' she said impatiently, and Alex gave a choked laugh and kissed her as he went on undressing her. 'And now,' he said, when she lay naked in his arms, 'for the rest of you.'

By the time Alex had finished kissing every inch of her better, they were both in such a high state of arousal that their lovemaking was too frantic to last long, and all too soon they lay clutching each other in the healing aftermath of the storm.

'So,' Alex said, when he could breathe again, 'are you better?'

'Not yet.' Sarah fought for breath. 'I shall need more of your medication, Doctor. Much more.'

Alex's eyes gleamed down into hers, the light in them changing to something that turned her heart over. 'I've missed you like hell, Sarah. Can you imagine how I felt when I found Dan Mason's car here when I gave in and came to see you? I wanted to break his jaw.'

'You'll have to stand in line. I'm going to break it first. But let's forget Dan.' She touched a caressing hand to his face. 'I've missed you, too.'

'Even though I'm a Merrick?'

'I told you—I'm over that.'

'Even though you thought I'd tried to queer your pitch at Westhope Farm?'

'I've apologised twice. Once by letter, and once face to face. But,' she added, her eyes kindling, 'I refuse to grovel any more.'

'It wasn't a very warm letter,' he said, smoothing the tumbled curls from her face.

'It took me ages. I was hoping,' she said tartly, 'for a reply.'

'Fond hope! I didn't take kindly to the accusations you flung at me, Sarah.' He scowled down at her. 'It was the final straw when I found you playing darts with your pals at the pub. Though, to be honest, I didn't go there just to look for you. I wanted Dan Mason's London address.'

Sarah propped herself up on an elbow in sudden suspicion. 'Why?'

'To pay him a visit.' Alex piled the cushions up and drew her down against them. 'Dan was notorious for playing nasty little tricks on people in school. Usually on defenceless types who couldn't retaliate. This time he chose the wrong target. Though he knew damn well I wouldn't report him to the police.'

'Why not?'

'No money was actually involved, and he could have passed off the rest as a joke that didn't come off.' Alex's smile turned Sarah's blood cold. 'So I waited for him to come home from work one evening, and pushed him back inside his smart loft the moment he opened the door. When I confronted him about the Westhope farce he started blustering, then suddenly lost it and punched me in the nose,' he added casually.

Sarah whistled. 'I can't see you turning the other cheek, so you must be the one who blacked his eye!'

'Oh, yes,' he said with relish. 'Don't worry. I didn't damage him much. Dan's main worry, the fool, was the blood on his jacket courtesy of my nose.'

She shook her head in wonder. 'I heard about a mugging. In the pub they think Dan was set on by a crowd of thugs.'

'He *would* say that,' said Alex, with scorn. 'The worst part was his stream of invective when I forced him to tell me why he did it. Apparently he hates me because my family's money got me the pick of the girls at Medlar House. Not my personal charm, you note. My other crime was my prowess at cricket and rugby, and winning too many events at Sports Day.' Alex shrugged. 'I pointed out that academically he'd won far more glittering prizes than me, but brains, as he spat at me, are no match for brawn when it comes to attracting women.'

Sarah's lip curled in disgust. 'Dan needs to grow up. It's a long time since you were both in school!'

'You're to blame for reviving his old animosity. He's convinced you were attracted to my family money.' Alex smiled crookedly and drew her close. 'Whereas, unknown to Dan, my name and all it stands for did me no good at all where you're concerned.'

Sarah shifted a little. 'This floor is hard, duvet or not, Alex.'

Alex promptly got up and pulled her to her feet. 'And I must go. Mother's leaving early in the morning.' He held her close as she tried to break away to pick up her clothes. 'Not so fast. We haven't discussed next weekend yet.'

'And we're not going to before I get some clothes on!'

When they were dressed, Alex sat down on the sofa and pulled Sarah on his knee. 'After I see Mother off I'm driving to London to sort out some problems with our restoration work on a riverside warehouse. My father and I have differing ideas on the subject, so I'll have to stay down for a few days to put him right.'

Sarah's lips twitched. 'Or he could put *you* right.'

Alex shook his head. 'He always comes round to my way of thinking in the end.'

'So when will you be back?'

'Friday night. So drive over first thing on Saturday morning. Please?' he added belatedly, and kissed her.

'Saturday afternoon,' she said firmly. 'I do things on Saturday morning.'

'Do them with me.'

'I'm talking about food-shopping and laundry,' she said, laughing.

Alex sighed. 'All right, if you must. Saturday afternoon, then.' He set Sarah on her feet and put his arm round her as they went to the door. 'Goodnight. Don't work too hard tomorrow. I'll ring you after dinner.' He kissed her, held her close for a moment, then gave her the crooked smile she'd missed so much. 'Sweet dreams.'

If Sarah did dream she remembered nothing about it next morning, after the best night's sleep she'd had in ages. And instead of her usual Monday morning reluctance, she approached work with a zest she knew Harry was wary of commenting on in case her mood changed. For once she ate all her portion of cottage pie at lunch, and even accepted a piece of the cake Ian's mother had sent with him for their tea break.

'Ian's reach will come in handy with the membrane on the highest bits,' she told Harry on the way home.

'Reach is one thing you lack, boss,' he said, lips twitching.

'I know. So you two can deal with the membrane. I'll put the cob fixings in to secure it,' she said briskly. 'When the first barn is finished I'll get going with the plastering, while you two put the membrane up in the others.'

'Have you been taking some vitamin pills or something?' asked Harry. 'You're in a very good mood today.'

'Are you suggesting I'm a bit hard to get on with some days?' she demanded.

'Yes,' he said bluntly. 'But so am I. Which is why we work well together, boss.'

Sarah had just finished supper when Alex rang that evening.

'Reporting in,' he said. 'Had a good day?'

'A wonderful day,' she told him. 'Did your mother get away on time this morning?'

'She did. And sent you her love. *Love*, not regards, she emphasised. 'You two really hit it off.'

'We certainly did. I like your mother very much, Alex.'

'Me too. I miss her when she goes back to Stratford. I'll need a lot of loving care from you, Sarah, to console me.'

'I'll see what I can do.'

Alex heaved a sigh. 'It's going to be a long week. Did I mention bringing an overnight bag with you on Saturday?'

'No.' Though Sarah had intended to anyway.

'If I only get you at weekends, Sarah Carver, that means from the moment you get to my place until first thing on Monday morning. Understood?'

'Understood.'

'And the following week I expect the weekend to start on Friday evening,' he informed her. 'I don't care how tired you are. You can doze the evening away on my sofa if you want. No need to drive. I'll fetch you, and drive you back on Monday morning. Do you approve my plan?'

'I just love your plan,' she said, and, since there was silence on the line for a moment, concluded she'd rendered him speechless.

On the way back to Medlar House the following Friday, Sarah was in such high spirits that Harry cast her a sly look

'Got a date tonight?'

'Not tonight. Tomorrow.'

'Good for you. All work and no play's a bad thing at your age.'

'Any age, Harry. So you have a good weekend too.'

Normally Sarah felt so weary on Friday evenings that she was too tired to do anything other than shower, eat and go to bed early with a book. This Friday she felt totally different. Probably because she'd been eating properly all week. And talking to Alex every night. So, instead of wasting part of her Saturday on cleaning and laundry she got on with it straight away, so she could turn up early next day at Glebe Barn as a surprise.

When Alex rang later, she told him he sounded tired.

'I am—whereas you sound full of beans, Sarah.'

'It's been a good week. We've got a lot done. I can now enjoy my weekend with a clear conscience.'

'With me.'

'With you.'

'I can't wait.' He yawned. 'I'm halfway home. I stopped at a service station for coffee to get me through the rest of the journey.'

'For heaven's sake, drive carefully!'

'You sound as though you care.'

'I do.'

'So do I,' he said softly. 'See you tomorrow, darling. Come as early as you can.'

Next morning Sarah did her shopping at the Post Office stores, rather than waste precious time driving miles to a supermarket. When she got back she put the food away, collected her overnight bag, and set off as she was, in jeans and a white cotton shirt, smiling as she pictured Alex's face when she turned up earlier than expected.

But when she arrived at Glebe Barn she found another car there before her, parked alongside Alex's Cherokee. A Porsche, Sarah noted, eyebrows raised. As she got out of the car she heard voices raised at the rear of the house. Helen had told her Alex was doing something in his garden this weekend. Apparently he had help. Female help.

Sarah went round the side of the house, then froze at the sight of a woman in Alex's arms. With a gasp, she turned tail and fled. But her feet crunched on the pebbles, and before she could reach her car Alex caught her.

'Sarah, it's not what you think.' He pulled her close and kissed her very thoroughly. 'You don't know how glad I am to see you,' he said, with feeling.

'Are you?' she said breathlessly.

'Yes. Thank God you came early. Come on.' He led her round to the patio he was building at the back. The woman stood there, tapping an impatient foot. She was tall and slender, with suspiciously voluptuous breasts, and straight blonde hair which framed a stunningly beautiful face.

Alex tightened his arm round Sarah as he introduced her. 'Sarah Carver, meet Maxine Merrick—my father's second wife.'

Help, thought Sarah. And what an odd way for Alex to describe his stepmother. 'How do you do?'

'Hello,' said Maxine curtly, and stabbed a look at Alex. 'Could we speak in private before I go, please? I'm running late.'

'Then take off right now,' said Alex. 'We have nothing more to say.'

Maxine looked at him with such venom that Sarah felt an absurd impulse to stand in front of him, like a bodyguard. 'I'm warning you, Alex, you'll regret this.'

'Oh, for God's sake, don't be such a drama queen, Max,' he said, bored.

Angry colour flared in her face. She slung her expensive bag over her shoulder and, ignoring Sarah, stalked past Alex on her way back to her car, throwing him a look so vicious it turned Sarah cold.

When the Porsche roared into life Alex turned Sarah into his arms, holding her so close she could feel his heart thudding against her. 'As wicked stepmothers go, Maxine takes the prize,' he said, rubbing his cheek against hers. 'Did you hear any of that?'

'No. I didn't wait long enough to hear any conversation.' She gave him a wry look. 'Seeing you with a woman in your arms was a horrible shock.'

'Maxine was trying her famed feminine wiles on me to persuade me into doing what she wanted.' Alex took her hand to lead her inside. 'I need coffee.'

They drank it close together on one of the deep, comfortable sofas. Alex was so obviously in need of the physical contact as much as the caffeine that Sarah kept quiet, leaving it to him to explain the incident. Or not.

'The delightful Maxine,' he said at last, 'came here this

morning to extort money from me. At this point I should tell you that she was once engaged to me—'

'So she's the one?' And Maxine had married his *father*?

Alex eyed her in surprise. 'Did Mother give you any details?'

'Only that someone hurt you badly. Helen thought it would explain you to me.'

'She's right. Maxine made me very wary of getting close to a woman again. Until I met you, Sarah.' He kissed her swiftly. 'Just to make it crystal clear that I'm immune to Maxine's charms these days, I'll tell you the entire sordid story.'

'You don't have to,' said Sarah quickly.

'I do, my darling. And even though it involves my mother, she strongly urged me to put you in the picture.' Alex took in a deep breath. 'There's no easy way of saying this. Mother told me, with great reluctance, that when she turned up unexpectedly at their London flat one day, she found my father enjoying some afternoon delight in their bed. His naked partner in crime was my fiancée, Maxine Rogers.'

Sarah stared at him in utter horror. 'How horrible! What on earth did Helen do?'

'She walked out without a word, and kept on walking—right out of my father's life. The worst part, she said, was explaining to me.'

'I can well believe that!' Sarah shuddered and held him close.

'It hit me for six,' said Alex huskily. 'My world came apart at the seams for a while.' He smiled evilly. 'But, being a true Merrick, I put it back together on my own terms. I can be as ruthless as old Edgar any day. My father ranted and raged in the beginning, but I wouldn't budge. And because he was suffering agonies of guilt he agreed to my terms in the end. So he remains as nominal chairman of the group, and runs the retail end from the London office, but I actually rule over the Merrick Group as a whole.'

'Did that make it easier to cope with the situation?'

'It helped. But I would have coped a lot better if Maxine's

lover had been anyone but my father. That was the pill I found
so bloody impossible to swallow.' Alex raked a hand through
his hair. 'By then I didn't care about Maxine, but I couldn't
understand how my father could do such a thing—to my
mother, I mean, not me.'

'I can't either. She's so lovely. And she looks far too young
to be your mother,' said Sarah. 'When did all this happen?'

'Six years ago. Mother looked even younger then. As far
as I know my father had never looked at another woman until
I brought Maxine home,' he said in disgust. 'When I learned
the truth my first instinct was to get as far away from my
father and the Merrick Group as I could. But once I'd cooled
down I realised I'd be a bloody fool to throw my birthright
away over a woman I no longer even cared for. My whole life
had been geared to taking over one day, so I simply informed
my father that the day had come sooner than planned, and
there was no room at the top for both of us. When my grandfather weighed in on my side my father caved in and agreed
to relocate to London.'

'And married Maxine?'

'After the divorce came through, yes.' Alex's smile turned
Sarah's blood cold. 'Maxine thought she'd fallen in the honey
pot. My father's a fit, good-looking man, and wealthy. He
bought her a penthouse flat in Chelsea, and—best of all to
Maxine—she wasn't required to ruin her figure with the
children I'd wanted. But things haven't worked out quite as
flawlessly for her as she'd hoped. My father is a canny man.
He'll give her anything her heart desires, lets her use her credit
card as much as she likes, but he checks the bill and pays it for
her. Lack of hard cash is her problem, and right now she needs
some in a hurry.'

'Has she run up some kind of debt?'

'No.' His mouth twisted in distaste. 'She wants the money for
a discreet abortion, plus a holiday with her mother afterwards in
some spa-type hotel in the sun to recuperate, without my father

being any the wiser. Then she'll return, pampered and massaged and good as new, to the arms of her unsuspecting husband.'

Sarah shook her head in wonder. 'But if your father doesn't want children why doesn't she just ask *him* for the money?'

Alex smiled evilly. 'My mother had such a bad time when I was born he had a vasectomy.'

Sarah winced. 'So Maxine has a lover?'

He shrugged. 'She went to a friend's party while my father was away on a business trip. She says she drank too much champagne, can't remember much about the evening, and now she's pregnant with no idea who's responsible.'

'Do you believe that?'

'Of course not. The man is probably someone else's cheating husband, who either refuses to take the blame or can't put up the money. And whatever Maxine feels—or doesn't feel—for my father, she's too much in love with the luxury he wraps her in to risk her marriage.'

Sarah shivered in distaste, and Alex drew her closer.

'Forget about Maxine. I've been looking forward to this weekend too much to let her spoil it for us.' He kissed her, then eyed her accusingly. 'You were supposed to bring an overnight bag!'

'I did. I left it in the car.'

'Give me your keys and I'll fetch it for you, then I'll get cleaned up and we'll eat.' He smiled and brushed a hand over her hair. 'I wasn't expecting a lunch guest, but I'm sure we can find something.'

Sarah went up to Alex's bedroom with him to unpack her bag, her eyebrows raised when she saw a new plasma television screen mounted on the wall opposite the bed.

'Wow!'

Alex grinned as he dumped her bag down. 'For entertainment on the lonely evenings you won't spend with me.'

'How many evenings have you been home alone this week?' she demanded.

'None. Because I was in London, working. I had this installed when you dumped me.'

'You mean when you dumped *me* because I wouldn't agree to your terms!' She glared at him, and he laughed, holding up his hands in surrender.

'Pax! No fighting before lunch.'

'All right,' she sighed, and melted into his arms. 'I've been looking forward to this all week.'

'So have I.' Alex kissed her hungrily, then with a sigh let her go. 'I need a shower, but I'll only be a minute so don't go away. Unpack your bag while I get clean.'

Sarah felt utterly happy as she unpacked in Alex's bedroom while he sang—quite well, she noticed—in the shower. There was an intimacy about it she liked a lot. And Alex's bedroom had a lot more going for it than her own place when it came to comfort. A thrill of pure delight ran through her at the thought of sharing the bed with Alex.

She smiled at him so radiantly as he emerged from the bathroom that he caught her in his arms.

'What were you thinking just then?'

'Just that I'd be sharing that bed with you tonight.'

He hugged her close, burying his face in her hair. 'If you're very good it's just possible I might let you share it with me this afternoon, too. An afternoon nap would do you good.'

'Would I sleep?'

'No. Do you want to?'

She pressed her lips against his warm, bare skin, exulting at the feel of his heartbeat against her mouth. 'No,' she whispered. 'I want you to make love to me, to make up for all the misery you've caused me.'

'I was miserable too,' he said, his arms tightening. 'Let's start making up for it right now—'

She wriggled away, laughing up at him. 'Not before I've eaten. I'm hungry.'

* * *

The weekend was everything Sarah had looked forward to—right through to the last moment when Alex kissed her goodbye at a brutally early hour on the Monday morning.

'Next week,' he said imperiously, 'you bring your work clothes and drive to Westhope from here.'

'Yes, Alex,' she said meekly, and spoiled the effect by sticking her tongue out at him.

He grinned and bent to kiss her. 'I do so like an obedient woman.'

'Then go find one,' she said, laughing, and kissed him back. 'Are you free on Wednesday evening, by any chance?'

His eyes narrowed to familiar gleam. 'I could be. Why?'

'The weekend is a long way away,' she said, looking up from under her eyelashes.

'Are you by any chance trying to say you'd like to see me before then?'

Sarah nodded eagerly. 'Not to go out. I *do* get tired, Alex. But if you fancy coming to my place for supper, I—I'd like that. Very much.'

Alex held her in such a punishing embrace that she protested against the lips crushing hers. 'Of course I fancy it,' he said roughly when he let her go, and brushed her hair back with a possessive hand. 'I longed to suggest it myself. But, having learned my lesson the hard way, I held my tongue.' He smiled into her eyes. 'Thank you, my darling.'

'Don't mention it,' she said, not quite lightly. 'About eight, then?'

'Don't cook. I'll bring something.'

To Sarah the time seemed to fly by for the next couple of days as she helped the men reline the barns.

'I'll be able to start plastering soon,' she said with satisfaction, as they finished in good time on the Wednesday.

'And how do you reckon you'll reach the top of this lot?' said Harry, indicating the height of the walls.

'Like Michelangelo did for the Sistine Chapel—with ladders and a trestle to stand on. Though I won't need to lie on my back, like him.'

Ian looked at her doubtfully. 'Couldn't you let my uncle do the top bits, boss, and you do the bottom halves?'

Harry shook his head. 'You'd see the difference.' He gave his nephew a fierce glare. 'Don't you ever let on I said this, but she's better at it than I am.'

'Harry actually admitted it,' crowed Sarah to Alex later, as they made inroads on the lasagne he'd coaxed out of Stephen. 'But he's much better at carpentry than I am, so I'm really lucky to have him for the banisters and stairs and so on.'

'And you've got his nephew for the brute strength department. You three make a formidable trio.' Alex helped her to more of the lasagne, then put the rest on his plate. 'Stephen would like you to know that takeout meals are not normally part of the Pheasant's repertoire. In other words, don't tell anyone he's doing us a special favour.'

'Which he does because he's your good friend,' agreed Sarah.

Alex dropped a kiss on her nose. 'And because he approves of you. Highly.'

'That's nice! Did he approve of Maxine?'

'No, because she upset his wife.' Alex grimaced. 'I met Maxine for the first time at Stephen's wedding. She's Jane's cousin, which means that Jane, no matter how much I or my mother try to persuade her otherwise, feels responsible for the mayhem Maxine caused.'

'I can sympathise with her,' said Sarah soberly.

'One more thing, and then let's delete Maxine from the evening. My father flew to New York last weekend, and for once Maxine didn't seize the chance to go with him. Instead she drove to the Pheasant to ask Jane for money.' Alex's eyes hardened. 'Steve turned her down flat. They're still getting established, and just don't have that kind of spare cash. Maxine took off in a temper and came to me—as you saw—then still with no luck, went running to her mother, who never has two pennies to rub together, so I don't suppose she had much luck there, either.'

'So what will she do now?'

He smiled, and rubbed his cheek against hers. 'Frankly, Scarlett, I don't give a damn. So forget Maxine and tell me what you'd like to do next weekend.'

'The same as last weekend,' said Sarah promptly. 'I'll help you finish your patio.'

'No, you won't. You can recline on a deckchair and hand out advice and instructions while *I* finish it. Then you can scrub my back in the bath afterwards. Or any other part of me you think needs attention,' he added with a grin. 'I'll pick you up here at seven. If you're not too tired we'll take a detour to monitor progress on the new hotel, and you can take a look at your cottages at the same time.'

'I won't be too tired for that,' she assured him, and knew she wouldn't be. The weariness of the past few weeks had been due to Alex Merrick's absence from her life. Her energy was fully restored now he was back in it again.

Sarah had just waved goodbye to Harry the following evening when she saw, with sinking heart, a familiar Porsche in the Medlar House car park. Maxine Merrick slid out of it, eyeing Sarah's work clothes with a patronising smile.

'Hello. Have you got a minute? I'd like a word,' said Maxine.

'How did you know where I live?' asked Sarah, making no attempt to hide her hostility.

'Apparently Alex went on *ad nauseam* about this flat of yours to Stephen, so I asked Stephen where it was. Can I come in?'

Sarah's first instinct was to refuse, but after a pause her curiosity got the better of her. She unlocked the outer door and strode across the hall to her flat, then stood aside to let her unwelcome visitor in.

'Heavenly little place,' said Maxine, looking round in surprise.

'Thank you. Why are you here?' Sarah asked bluntly.

'To give you a friendly warning,' said Maxine, her china-blue eyes limpid.

'What exactly are you warning me about, Mrs Merrick?'

'Alex, and how ruthless he can be,' said Maxine, sighing. 'May I sit down?'

Sarah shook her head. 'I've had a long day, and I need a shower. I'd rather you just said what you have to say and go.'

Maxine's mouth tightened. 'All right then, Miss Carver. To get straight to the point, I think it's only right you know that Alex got me pregnant out of revenge, to hurt his father. You probably heard some of that when you walked in on us last Saturday. One look at you gave me the perfect lever I needed. I threatened to tell you everything unless Alex paid up for an abortion. Which he did, finally, but I'm telling you anyway, just to enjoy the feeling.' Her eyes hardened to chips of blue ice. 'No man tells me to get lost and gets away with it. Why are you shaking your head like that?' she added with sudden hostility.

'I feel so sorry for him,' said Sarah.

'Alex?' snapped Maxine.

'No. For his father.' Sarah flung the door wide. 'Goodbye, Mrs Merrick.'

'Hold on, I haven't finished—'

'Yes, you have. Take your lies and leave, or I'll call the caretaker.' Sarah smiled sweetly. 'To quote Alex, Mrs Merrick, get lost.'

Maxine turned a deep, unbecoming crimson, speechless with fury for a moment, but before she could recover Sarah thrust her out into the hall and closed the door, her heart beating like a drum.

Alex arrived fifteen minutes early the following evening. 'Sorry,' he said, kissing Sarah, 'I couldn't wait any longer. If you're not ready, I'll wait until you are.'

'Harry needed to get away a bit earlier today, so I was home in good time,' she assured him, and pointed to her bags. 'If you'll take those to the car, I'll just lock up.'

'Yes, ma'am!' he said with alacrity, and looked her over with appreciation. 'You look good enough to eat, Sarah.'

She smiled and reached up to kiss him. 'So do you.'

When they called in at the hotel construction site Sarah took a nostalgic look at the row of cottages.

'Note the trees,' said Alex, watching her face. 'I had the rest of the houses planted up to match the first one. You approve?'

'I do. I'm flattered you liked my taste. My cottages look really good. I'll always think of them as mine, you know,' she added, smiling.

'So will I.' Alex kissed her swiftly as he helped her down. 'I'm very glad, now, that you refused my original offer.'

'I should think I would,' she said indignantly. 'It was outrageous.'

'I meant the one I made before you even left London to start work on them,' he said, and sprang back, hands upraised in mock surrender.

Sarah stared at him blankly. 'That was you?'

He nodded, smiling broadly. 'I told the manager of one of our London subsidiaries to put out a feeler for me. When you didn't bite I decided to sit back and let you get on with them.'

She laughed in disbelief. 'You devious devil! Why didn't you tell me this before?'

He laid a hand on his heart. 'Harmony has not been a continuous feature of our relationship, Miss Carver, so I waited until it was on firmer ground before I confessed.'

'Good thinking.' Sarah blew him a kiss. 'Now, show me over this hotel and then take me home. I'm hungry.'

They were in bed together later that night, wrapped in each other's arms in the afterglow of making love, before she dropped her bombshell.

'I had a visitor last night,' she said, as Alex stroked her hair.

'If it was Dan Mason I'll black his other eye!'

'It was Maxine.'

Alex shot upright, his eyes incredulous as he stared down into Sarah's flushed face. 'What the hell did she want?'

'To make trouble for you, Alex.'

'What else is new?' he said grimly. 'What particular brand of trouble did she dish out this time?'

'She said you gave her the money for her abortion.'

Alex took in a deep breath, then caught her in his arms, his eyes looking deep into hers. 'I didn't give her any money, Sarah. I haven't seen her since last Saturday.'

'I know, darling,' she said gently.

He let out the breath, and rubbed his cheek against hers. 'I realise that, now my brain's started functioning again, otherwise you wouldn't be here with me like this—wouldn't have let me through your door tonight.'

'I believed the worst of you without evidence once, Alex,' she said firmly. 'I wasn't going to do it a second time. I did think for a fleeting moment you might have given her the money to spare your father. But her big mistake was saying you'd made her pregnant—'

'*What?*'

'Precisely. After what happened with your mother I knew you wouldn't touch Maxine again with a bargepole.'

'How right you are.' Alex crushed her close again in gratitude. 'You trusted me.'

'Yes, I did.' She smiled up at him. 'I do.'

His own smile was crooked as he returned the smile. 'I like the sound of that.'

'That I trust you?'

'No. The "I do" bit.'

Sarah swallowed, trying to control her somersaulting heart. 'Where do you think she got the money?' she said hastily, in case she was taking too much for granted.

'Don't know, don't care. Maybe her mother came up trumps for once.' Alex paused. 'But Maxine must have got it somewhere if she came round to you to gloat and spit out lies. Though I didn't think even she would be that vindictive.'

'You told her to get lost. She couldn't take that.'

'It's probably never happened to her before.'

'It has twice now.' Sarah smiled victoriously. 'I told her to get lost, too.'

Alex gave a crow of laughter, then grew quiet. 'Thank you, Sarah,' he said at last.

'For telling Maxine to get lost?'

'No, though I wish I'd been there to witness it. My thanks are for trusting me, Merrick though I am.' He held her close in silence for a while, then turned her face up to his. 'Talking of which, I've thought of a foolproof way of getting you used to my name.'

'Oh?'

'If you moved in here with me, and got gradually used to the idea, we could get married—preferably some time soon— and then your name would be Merrick, too. I know,' he added hastily, as her jaw dropped, 'that certain of my relatives leave something to be desired. But you've met my lovely Aunt Bel, and I think you'd even like old Edgar—and to crown it all you'd have the best mother-in-law in the business.'

'Are you serious?' she said, even as a glow of pure happiness spread through her.

'About my mother? Of course I am—'

'I mean about getting married.'

'Sarah,' said Alex patiently, 'you've worked among men all your life. You should know how they tick better than most women. Can you imagine any man saying something like that for a joke?'

'No, thank God!' She threw her arms round his neck in rapture at the thought of marrying Alex Merrick, whatever his name was.

'I wanted you the moment I set eyes on you—even when I thought you were Oliver Moore's trophy girlfriend,' he told her, and curled a lock of hair round his finger. 'Of course I didn't know then what trouble you'd cause me—'

'Trouble?' she said indignantly.

'False accusations for one,' he reminded her. 'You hurt me, my darling.'

'I know,' she said with remorse. 'I'm sorry, Alex.'

'But now you've trusted me rather than Maxine I feel I'm on a winning streak here. So how do you feel about marrying me, Sarah Carver?'

'Ecstatic,' she said, her smile incandescent. 'If I do, will you expect me to give up my work?'

'Hell, no,' he said fervently. 'Maybe you'll get so good at it I can retire early. I've always had a fancy to be a kept man.'

'Have you, now?'

'Well, no,' Alex admitted, kissing her. 'If there's any keeping involved I'd rather do it, because you'd have to have the babies.' He drew back to look her in the eye. 'Do you want children, Sarah?'

She nodded earnestly. 'Of course I do. As long as they're yours, Alex.'

He relaxed and held her closer. 'Then tell me I can keep you, Sarah.'

'Oh, yes,' she said with a blissful sigh. 'For ever, please. Besides, rather than shock Oliver, I'd prefer to marry you before we have these babies of ours.'

He rubbed his cheek against hers. 'I'll take all that as a yes, then.'

'A very enthusiastic one! I think your mother will be pleased.'

Alex laughed, and kissed her nose. 'You're only taking me on so you get my mother as well!'

'Of course. Though I love you madly, too.' She smiled suddenly, her eyes dancing. 'Oliver will be delighted, naturally, but I don't fancy telling Harry Sollers.'

'I'll break it to him myself. In the pub, so that all your pals hear the news at the same time.' Alex gave her his familiar crooked smile. 'And then, light of my life, I'll ask Eddy Mason to pass on the good news to Dan.'

* * * * *

Harlequin Presents® is thrilled to introduce sparkling new talent Caitlin Crews!
Caitlin's debut book is a fast-paced, intense story, with a gorgeous Italian hero, a defiant princess and plenty of passion and seduction!

Available next month in Harlequin Presents: PURE PRINCESS, BARTERED BRIDE

"YOU HAVE MADE him proud," he told her, nodding at her father, feeling benevolent. "You are the jewel of his kingdom."

Finally, she turned her head and met his gaze, her sea-colored eyes were clear and grave as she regarded him.

"Some jewels are prized for their sentimental value," she said, her musical voice pitched low, but not low enough to hide the faint tremor in it. "And others for their monetary value."

"You are invaluable," he told her, assuming that would be the end of it. Didn't women love such compliments? He'd never bothered to give them before. But Gabrielle shrugged, her mouth tightening.

"Who is to say what my father values?" she asked, her light tone unconvincing. "I would be the last to know."

"But I know," he said.

"Yes." Again, that grave, sea-green gaze. "I am invaluable, a jewel without price." She looked away. "And yet, somehow, contracts were drawn up, a price agreed upon and here we are."

There was the taint of bitterness to her words then. Luc frowned. He should not have indulged her—he regretted the impulse. This was what happened when emotions were given reign.

"Tell me, princess," he said, leaning close, enjoying the way her eyes widened, though she did not back away from him. He liked her show of courage, but he wanted to make his point perfectly clear. "What was your expectation? Do not speak to me of contracts and prices in this way, as if you are the victim of some subterfuge," he ordered her, harshly. "You insult us both."

Her gaze flew to his, and he read the crackling temper there. It intrigued him as much as it annoyed him—but either way he could not allow it. There could be no rebellion, no bitterness, no intrigue in this marriage. There could only be his will and her surrender.

He remembered where they were only because the band chose that moment to begin playing. He sat back in his chair, away from her. *She is not merely a business acquisition,* he told himself, once more grappling with the urge to protect her— safeguard her. *She is not a hotel, or a company.*

She was his wife. He could allow her more leeway than he would allow the other things he controlled. At least today.

"No more of this," he said, rising to his feet. She looked at him warily. He extended his hand to her and smiled. He could be charming if he chose. "I believe it is time for me to dance with my wife."

Indulge yourself with this passionate love story that starts out as a royal marriage of convenience, and look out for more dramatic books from Caitlin Crews and Harlequin Presents in 2010!

HARLEQUIN
Ambassadors

Want to share your passion for reading Harlequin® Books?

Become a Harlequin Ambassador!

Harlequin Ambassadors are a group
of passionate and well-connected readers
who are willing to share their joy of reading
Harlequin® books with family and friends.

You'll be sent all the tools you need to spark
great conversation, including free books!

All we ask is that you share the romance
with your friends and family!

You'll also be invited to have a say in
new book ideas and exchange opinions
with women just like you!

To see if you qualify* to be
a Harlequin Ambassador, please visit
www.HarlequinAmbassadors.com.

*Please note that not everyone who applies to be a Harlequin Ambassador will
qualify. For more information please visit www.HarlequinAmbassadors.com.

Thank you for your participation.

BAP09BPA

TWO CROWNS, TWO ISLANDS, ONE LEGACY

A royal family torn apart by pride and its lust for power, reunited by purity and passion

Harlequin Presents is proud to bring you the
final installment from The Royal House of Karedes.
As the stories unfold, secrets and sins from the past
are revealed and desire, love and passion war
with royal duty!

Look for:

THE DESERT KING'S HOUSEKEEPER BRIDE
#2891

by Carol Marinelli
February 2010

LARGER-PRINT BOOKS!

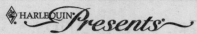

GET 2 FREE LARGER-PRINT
NOVELS PLUS 2 FREE GIFTS!

YES! Please send me 2 FREE LARGER-PRINT Harlequin Presents® novels and my 2 FREE gifts (gifts are worth about $10). After receiving them, if I don't wish to receive any more books, I can return the shipping statement marked "cancel". If I don't cancel, I will receive 6 brand-new novels every month and be billed just $4.55 per book in the U.S. or $5.24 per book in Canada. That's a saving of 13% off the cover price! It's quite a bargain! Shipping and handling is just 50¢ per book in the U.S. and 75¢ per book in Canada.* I understand that accepting the 2 free books and gifts places me under no obligation to buy anything. I can always return a shipment and cancel at any time. Even if I never buy another book, the two free books and gifts are mine to keep forever.

176 HDN E4GC   376 HDN E4GN

Name	(PLEASE PRINT)

Address	Apt. #

City	State/Prov.	Zip/Postal Code

Signature (if under 18, a parent or guardian must sign)

Mail to the **Harlequin Reader Service:**
IN U.S.A.: P.O. Box 1867, Buffalo, NY 14240-1867
IN CANADA: P.O. Box 609, Fort Erie, Ontario L2A 5X3

Not valid for current subscribers to Harlequin Presents Larger-Print books.

**Are you a subscriber to Harlequin Presents books
and want to receive the larger-print edition?
Call 1-800-873-8635 today!**

* Terms and prices subject to change without notice. Prices do not include applicable taxes. Sales tax applicable in N.Y. Canadian residents will be charged applicable provincial taxes and GST. Offer not valid in Quebec. This offer is limited to one order per household. All orders subject to approval. Credit or debit balances in a customer's account(s) may be offset by any other outstanding balance owed by or to the customer. Please allow 4 to 6 weeks for delivery. Offer available while quantities last.

Your Privacy: Harlequin Books is committed to protecting your privacy. Our Privacy Policy is available online at www.eHarlequin.com or upon request from the Reader Service. From time to time we make our lists of customers available to reputable third parties who may have a product or service of interest to you. If you would prefer we not share your name and address, please check here. ☐

Help us get it right—We strive for accurate, respectful and relevant communications. To clarify or modify your communication preferences, visit us at www.ReaderService.com/consumerschoice.

PREGNANT BRIDES

*Inexperienced and expecting,
they're forced to marry!*

Bestselling Harlequin Presents author

Lynne Graham

brings you the second story
in this exciting new trilogy:

RUTHLESS MAGNATE, CONVENIENT WIFE
#2892
Available February 2010

Also look for

GREEK TYCOON, INEXPERIENCED MISTRESS
#2900
Available March 2010

www.eHarlequin.com

HP12892